Hairspray Horror

A PRIDE STREET PARANORMAL COZY MYSTERY
BOOK FOUR

T. THORN COYLE

Pride Street

CHAPTER 1
Marsha

IT WAS HOT. Like, I barely wanted to touch the sidewalk hot. Even the big elm trees lining Pride Street didn't cast enough shade to help my poor paws. What's a corgi to do?

Lie down. So, I did.

I panted next to Klaus beneath a four-top picnic table outside Bruiser's Best Beans. When I'd tried to go inside the café, John and Garret said no. That word was followed by some nonsense about it being too nice outside to sit indoors. I swear, sometimes humans are ridiculous.

"Klaus! Stop touching me! You're too hot!"

The blond corgi whined. *"Then scoot over! Why do you get all the shade?"*

"I don't." Even though I deserved more shade. My black fur was much hotter than Klaus's tan and white. Being a tricolor corgi made me more beautiful, but beauty has a price.

I whuffed meaningfully at Bruiser who was the largest of us three, and the one actually taking up the bulk of the shade. Why hadn't John and Garret tied us to one of the big elm trees instead of parking us beneath a table? Ugh.

Bruiser, a black and white spotted bulldog with a smashed in face, farted in answer. Gross. That dog needed some serious dietary changes. Luckily, a breeze waved his fart away and replaced the scent with the smell of roasted coffee beans and baked goods. Much more pleasant.

"Hey, my dogs, what's good?" a familiar human voice asked.

"What's good? What's good?" That was definitely a squawk I recognized.

I lifted my weary head and poked my nose out from beneath the table. Sure enough, walking toward us was Ron, the owner of Bones, Dogs, and Harmony, the Pride Street pet supply and record store. His super mellow black lab, Fred, ambled at his side. The very noisy Josephine Baker, an opinionated African Gray parrot, rode on one shoulder.

Despite the heat, Ron was in his usual uniform of a T-shirt with some sort of writing on it beneath an open, short sleeve cotton shirt. Today's had orange stripes which looked nice against his dark skin.

Josephine Baker preened one of the long, coiled locs that fell over his shoulders. Just looking at all of Ron's hair made me even hotter. My own tri-color, mostly black coat was at least short. Sort of.

Fred slumped down against one of the sidewalk trees with a huff and dropped his head to crossed paws.

"You guys needs more water?" Ron asked, checking out the bowls between the wood tables.

"*Yes!*" Klaus woofed. "*And some treats!*"

"*Treats!*" I echoed. A corgi has her priorities.

Ron laughed. "I'll take that as a yes. Back in a sec."

"Any news from the shop?" I asked Fred. Unlike Garret's store, which didn't get a lot of browsers, Fred and Ron's record and pet store was a community hub. If a human didn't have an animal, they at least liked music, so Fred got visitors on a regular basis.

And visitors meant gossip.

"The muffin shop has a new line of baked dog treats…" Fred began.

My ears perked up at that, and so did Klaus's. Maybe we could convince John and Garrett to drop by before we went home. Or maybe Bruiser's was already carrying them!

"…and Tracy at the convenience store got two new kittens. They're kind of dumb and clumsy, but cute."

That wasn't the world's most interesting gossip, but a corgi will take what she can get.

I heard John's voice. Finally. He and Garrett loped out of the coffee shop carrying a variety of drinks and plates. Ron followed behind them, balancing two water bowls and a fidgeting Josephine Baker.

Klaus leapt up and barked excitedly.

"Are those treats? Are there treats? Are they the new treats from the muffin shop?"

Garrett laughed and John gave Klaus one of his *I'm acting like I'm angry but I'm not really* looks.

"Settle down, little man," Ron said, setting one water bowl near my prancing friend, and scooting one under the table in the shade.

Klaus is excitable and not very smart, but he has a good heart, so I love him. I am also more beautiful than Klaus and remind him of that fact as often as I can.

Klaus yipped until Garrett took pity on him and shoved a treat in his mouth.

"Holy kamoley, this is delicious," Klaus chewed and barked, crumbs flying from his mouth and hitting me in the face.

"Watch it, you slob!" My bark was sharp, and Klaus's eyes got big in his head. But his mouth was open, and I could see half-chewed biscuit on his tongue. *"Close your mouth when you chew!"*

He snapped his jaws shut.

"Here you go, Marsha," Garrett said, holding out a bone-shaped brown biscuit. I sniffed it, then snapped it between my teeth.

Dang. Klaus was right. These new treats were fantastic. My tail wagged as if it was possessed. I couldn't stop it, and I didn't even want to. Fred, Klaus, and I all flopped down to finish eating. Which didn't take long. That's the trouble with treats. They go so quickly.

I hate that.

Klaus lapped at some water as Josephine Baker paced the edge of the picnic table, bobbing her gray feathered head. People walked by, pushing strollers or holding hands. A group of bicyclists rode past, but I was too worn out from the heat to even bark, let alone try to chase after them.

Above us, the humans enjoyed their own treats and drank the disgusting brew that they all loved. Garrett was talking about a new design client and Ron asked John about his latest thriller. John writes books, pounding away on his computer in an office at home.

"I'm bored," Klaus whined after we'd lain there, panting, for a while. *"Can't we go do something interesting?"*

"It's too hot to do something interesting," I replied. I mean, I like adventure as much as the next dog, but right now?

All I wanted was to go back home, or to Garrett's shop, and laze around in some cool air.

"*Too hot,*" Bruiser agreed before farting.

"*Bruiser! Not in Fred's face!*" I barked. Fred just gave a mournful sigh and shook his black shaggy head, collar tags jingling.

"Hey, Garrett!" That was a new voice. "Hi, Ron!"

I poked my nose out from underneath the table and looked up at a man in white trousers and a pale shirt. He had dark skin like Ron's and even darker eyes and looked kind. I can always tell with humans. Well, mostly.

"Hi, Sebastian! This is my partner John. Unlike the rest of us who run respectable shops, John kills people for a living."

Sebastian's eyes grew huge as John held out a hand to shake.

"Nice to meet you, Sebastian. What Garrett means is I'm a thriller and mystery writer."

"Oh!" Sebastian laughed. "Good one, Garrett. I just took over the hair salon down the street. Looking Good. If you ever need a cut, I'm your man."

Klaus got up and sniffed at Sebastian's shoes, which were snowy white sneakers that looked like they got cleaned every day.

"*Better not get any slobber on those shoes,*" I barked.

"*They smell funny,*" Klaus replied, shaking his blond nose, then sneezing. Right on the shoes.

"And who is this?" Sebastian asked, stretching out a hand for Klaus to sniff. Klaus darted his head forward and back. Something was making him skittish, and I wanted to know what.

"The one who just sneezed on your brand-new sneakers is Klaus," John replied. "Let me know if they need to be cleaned. And that's Marsha, and Bruiser, and you've probably met Fred."

Humans. Something was clearly wrong with this Sebastian, according to Klaus's reaction, but they didn't even notice.

I sighed. It was too hot for a mystery, even for a sleuthing corgi like me.

CHAPTER 2

Garrett

"SEE YOU FOR DINNER, MY LOVE," John said, giving me a quick kiss. "You sure you're good to take the dogs?"

"It's fine," I said. "You're on deadline and Klaus and Marsha are just going to take a nap in the air conditioning no matter where they are. The dogs might as well come to the store."

"Okay," my handsome partner replied, giving me another kiss. I watched him walk away, his short, dark, straight hair shining in the late summer sun. He's a gorgeous one, my man John Tang. Tall, slender, with nicely defined muscles and gold-tinged skin he got from his Chinese-American parents. I'm short and pasty white with a soft belly, nearsighted eyes, and a sparkly brain. Sometimes I wonder why he loves me so much.

I'm just really glad he chose me, simple Garrett Henson—a slightly built trans man from rural Oregon—for his life partner. We haven't talked marriage yet, but the big Craftsman we own together feels like commitment enough. For now, at least.

"Well, I'd better get to the store," I said to Ron and Sebastian. "Come on dogs."

"Have a good day, Garrett. I'll be in about that vintage record player later," Ron said.

"Sounds good."

Klaus and Marsha both stood and stretched. I clipped leashes to collars, and weaving through the Saturday morning sidewalk crowd, headed toward the shop. Klaus and Marsha both turned their heads to look behind us.

"What's up, you two? Did you forget to say goodbye to Bruiser?"

But then I heard my name.

I stopped and turned. It was Sebastian, race walking after us, perspiration dotting his smooth broad forehead. He was one of those well-groomed people that made me feel like a schlub, despite my neatly pressed short sleeve shirt and navy chinos. Like, I thought I looked fine when I left the house, but now? I probably had a red face, my stylish tortoiseshell glasses were slipping down my nose, and my shirt had already begun to wilt.

My dandy style does much better autumn through winter, when I can wear my favorite vests and bow ties. Yeah. Summer and I do not get along.

"Sebastian? Is everything okay?"

He frowned at me. "I… I'm not sure. Can I talk to you while you open?"

He glanced down at his watch. "I don't have to open for another hour, and I really want to run something by you."

"Sure," I said, and resumed walking. Sebastian was silent as we walked along Pride Street under the big leafy elms and cherry trees with their dropped fruit staining the sidewalks. I'd learned to wait for people to talk, but that didn't mean I wasn't curious why a man I'd never met wanted to talk to me.

I tugged the dog's leashes, skirting around a clump of what looked like straight women who'd had one too many mimosas at brunch. There were a lot of people out enjoying the sunshine, and I hoped that meant a lot of browsers at Dandy Lion's Design and Decor. The shop was my pride and joy, and my design business was growing every month.

Which was good. John made a lot of money writing and indie publishing his thrillers, but I always wanted to pull my own weight. He'd helped me out when my business was a fledgling proposition, and I was happy things felt more equal now.

I mean, he still made more money than me, but I could spring for a lot more dog treats these days.

I unlocked the front door and entered the cool, hushed space.

"Come on in," I said, locking the door behind Sebastian and unclipping Klaus and Marsha from their leashes before flipping on the lights.

The two corgis raced around, sniffing, checking to make sure everything was as they'd last left it.

Pausing a moment, I scanned the store, making sure all was still in order myself, and smiled.

After years of designing my own spaces, I finally had a business to call my own, partially thanks to word of mouth, and partially the joys and sorrows of social media.

The shop had huge windows that lined the front and one side and was filled with carefully curated treasures from a variety of time periods. Currently, Victorian era furniture was in the back and to the right, next to the

Craftsman section, with other styles emerging as you got closer to the front.

I'd left Yarrow to close the night before and they'd done a great job of tidying and dusting the Art Deco furniture grouping near the front and the fabulous mid-mod section just behind it. It might be time to rearrange the space again. Keep things fresh. If customers always see the same thing when they enter the store, they think there's no new stock.

Sometimes you have to trick people into going further than two feet past the door.

I headed behind the tall wooden antique sideboard that served as our cash point and front office space and fired up the tablet as the dogs settled themselves on their beds in the front window. What can I say? I was not above using adorable dogs to lure customers into my lair.

Computer chores done, I finally looked at Sebastian, who sat on the swooping art deco sofa, jiggling the foot crossed over his knee. He was handling a black ceramic candlestick of a woman holding a vase on her shoulder, and I really hoped he didn't scratch the thing. It actually was worth a chunk of change.

"Are your sneakers okay?" I asked. "Klaus's sneezes can be deadly."

"What?" He jerked, setting the candlestick down on a side table with a thunk that made me wince. He looked down at his no longer pristine shoes. "Oh. Yeah. They'll be fine. Nothing a little Mr. Clean can't take care of."

Ah. Unlike me, he actually cleaned his shoes. No wonder they looked so good.

"Do you want tea?" I asked, inclining my head toward the curtained off area that held our shipping and stock room along with the toilet and a tiny kitchenette.

He shook his head and stared out the big plate glass windows lining two sides of the shop. I don't think he was looking at anything outside.

I sighed. Life had been calm these past few months, and I really wanted it to stay that way. But whatever was troubling Sebastian was about to be dumped on me. Don't get me wrong, I love helping people, but sometimes I just want to live an ordinary life, you know?

As ordinary a life as a gay trans man with two nosy corgis and a beautiful home haunted by a dead AIDS activist could be. Not to mention being partners with a handsome thriller writer, which was slightly unusual, too.

Well, nothing to be done for the situation now except ask the hairdresser what the heck was going on. I still had around ten minutes before official opening, so I wound my way around tables, chairs, and tchotkes and plopped my chinos into an overstuffed Deco era chair covered in burgundy velvet.

"What's on your mind?"

Sebastian said nothing. Okay.

"Look," I said. "It's clear something is upsetting you, but I'm not psychic. You either need to tell me what's up or let me get ready to open the store."

My design business was my big money maker, but the store was my bread and butter. I couldn't afford to not open on a sunny weekend day.

Sebastian rubbed his hands across his face, leaving his dark cheeks with a slightly reddish sheen. He exhaled noisily, as if he'd been underwater.

"I'm sorry," he said. "I just… don't know where to begin."

"Start anywhere. Just spit it out."

"I think someone is trying to sabotage Looking Good."

CHAPTER 3

Marsha

"SABOTAGE?" My ears perked up at the word. *"Did you hear that, Klaus! It sounds like we might have another case!"*

"Whuuuh?" Klaus snorted and jerked his head, flinging a string of drool across his bed.

"You're disgusting. And how'd you fall asleep so fast, we've been here for like, five minutes! Wake up and pay attention!"

My blond friend licked his snout and smacked his lips before finally focusing his brown eyes on Garrett and Sebastian who were still talking on the cozy furniture we were under no circumstances allowed to sit on. It was an unjust world we lived in, where humans were invited to sit on sofas, and we got shooed off.

"Should we move closer?" Klaus asked.

"That's just one of the strange things that's been going on," Sebastian was saying.

Dang. Sounded like we'd missed a clue!

"Yeah," I barked. *"Let's."*

Klaus waddled toward the end of the display window to the little set of stairs Garrett had set up for us. It made getting to our window beds much easier, let me tell you.

My legs are perfectly proportioned to my body, but getting down from anything over a foot or so is a bit much, even for an agile dog such as myself.

We both headed toward the chair where Garrett sat. He dangled a hand down and I shoved my head under it. But after a few random skritches, Garrett stopped. Sebastian was distracting him. I flopped down half underneath a glass-topped coffee table with a sigh. Klaus thumped down next to me.

"Things are... going missing?" Garrett asked. He sounded confused. "Are you sure someone didn't just put things away incorrectly?"

"That's what I thought at first, but the longer it went on, the more I started thinking it was sabotage. But yesterday..."

"*Yesterday what?*" I barked. I swear, sometimes it takes humans so long to get to the point. Didn't they know we had napping to do?

Sebastian leaned forward, hands on his knees. I could see him through the glass of the coffee table. His brow was furrowed like he was about to growl or something. Or, in human terms, like he was worried.

"Yesterday, someone switched the permanent activator and the color dye activator."

"Seems like an honest enough mistake to me," Garrett replied.

"A mistake that could seriously damage a person's hair and scalp." Sebastian's voice was somber.

"*That doesn't sound so good,*" Klaus whoofed. "*I wouldn't like having my fur damaged.*"

"*Hush,*" I barked, snapping at one of his golden paws.

"Settle down, you two," Garrett said, but I could tell his heart wasn't in it.

And it wasn't that I disagreed with Klaus, but now was not the time to discuss our fur. Even though mine was clearly more beautiful, and Klaus knew it.

We had clues to listen for.

"And you've talked with the other hairdressers about it? And any employees?"

"I talked with our cleaner and the nail tech, as well as the other two stylists. No one seemed to know anything about it. So I just reminded everyone to be more careful. We share the space and the products, and we need to work in a safe, congenial atmosphere. I can't go accusing someone of... what? Being careless? Inattentive? I mean, my partner has ADHD and sometimes puts the orange juice in the cupboard instead of the fridge, but it's never anything serious!"

"Sebastian, I know this feels serious to you, but..."

Uh oh. Even I knew that a human saying that to another human was not a good thing.

"Serious to me? Are you kidding? I wanted to talk to you because I thought you of all people would take me seriously, Garrett! I'm the new shop on the block, I get it. You don't exactly know me yet. But everyone around says you're as trustworthy as they come and that you've..."

"Helped people?" Garrett replied.

"Solved cases!" I yapped.

"That you've solved cases. Murder even."

Garrett was shifting in his chair the way he did when something was making him feel uncomfortable.

"I just don't see what I could do," he finally said.

Sebastian scrubbed his hands across his face. Both men just sat quietly, breathing.

"What are they doing?" Klaus asked. *"I thought there'd be more clues."*

I ignored my friend. I'd been around humans my whole life and knew that this kind of silence usually meant something important was about to happen.

"All I can tell you is I know in my gut something is wrong. Someone is trying to sabotage Looking Good. Would you at least come by the salon when you get a chance? Look around?"

"Sure," Garrett replied. "I could use a haircut anyway."

A knock came at the shop door. Both men jumped and Klaus and I raced toward the heavy glass door, barking in excitement. Customers meant head scratches and sometimes even treats.

"I'll… I'll let you get to work," Sebastian said. "I've got to open soon, too."

"I'll call and make an appointment," Garrett said, flipping the sign to Open and unlocking the door.

"Oh! Thank goodness!" Princess Sparkle Toes rushed in, almost crashing into Sebastian who had moved into position to exit. "I thought you'd never open!"

A pair of bright yellow chunky-heeled sandals with green painted toenails peeking out the fronts barely missed my nose. I yipped and jumped back, crashing into Klaus.

"Hey!" he barked. *"Watch out!"*

Sebastian found an opening and slid out the door.

"Who was that handsome man?" Princess Sparkle Toes asked, fanning her pale face with her hands, wafting rosewater scent everywhere. A gold, six-pointed star winked from the vee of a bright, daisy-covered short dress that matched the deadly sandals, and her face was painted as if she was headed to a fancy dinner or something. But that's just the way PST—as Garrett and John sometimes call her —looks.

I looked at her wrist, but there was no hamster purse dangling today, just a stack of bracelets. Too bad. I like Mr. Cheeks.

"Hello, Princess Sparkle Toes," Garrett said, bending down to make sure Klaus and I were both okay. He gave us each a good scratch, then stood up again. "That was Sebastian. He owns Looking Good."

"Ooh! The new hair salon! I've been meaning to make an appointment but I'm just so *busy* these days!"

Sparkle Toes co-ran a dog and cat clothing line and was always trying to get Klaus and I to model for free. I'm not the biggest fan of anything covering my glossy fur, but Klaus can be talked into pretty much anything that makes him the center of attention and involves treats after.

Garrett stepped behind the counter and started making his "I'm doing business now" motions. That usually meant moving pieces of paper from one pile to another one or poking at the shiny tablet on its little black stand while ignoring us.

"What brings you here today?"

"I thought you'd never ask!" Princess Sparkle Toes said. "You know that new drag queen at Enrico's?"

"Uhh… which one? John and I haven't made it there for a few weeks."

Sparkle Toes pouted her painted lips.

"I know, you two fuddy-duddies! I swear, you'd think you were both ancient or something! At any rate, there was a fabulous new queen named Poison Penny…"

"Wait," Garrett interrupted. "What do you mean, was? John and I just saw her perform a month ago!"

"That's what I've been trying to tell you! Poison Penny is dead!"

CHAPTER 4

Garrett

JOHN WAS COOKING, padding from stove to sink in his socks, his shock of black hair sticking up a bit in back. That was a dead giveaway that he'd had a tough writing session. He always tugged at his cowlick when his murderer du jour had painted the novel into a corner, and he didn't know how to get back out.

Give me customers, furniture, and interior design over making things up any day. Even when my design clients were persnickety, I could just switch out a lamp, chair, or wallpaper color and smooth things over. John had to figure things out just using his beautiful brain.

I was propped on a stool near the door to the dining room, enjoying the scent of rice in our small cooker and whatever John was stirring on the stove. Something fragrant with tomato and a bunch of spices. The dogs lounged near my feet, happy to be with their humans. Happy to be home.

We live in an old Craftsman-style home not far from Pride Street. It was haunted by the ghost of a former ACT-UP member, a leather daddy who apparently used to live here with a passel of other gay men. A far cry from our cozy domestic family life. I mean, we had the occasional dinner or garden party, but not the raging gatherings I'm certain used to grace these walls.

"How did Poison Penny die again?" John asked. I hopped off the stool and bent over the stove to look in the big pan. Aha. The amazing scent was savory braised tofu, green beans, and John's secret sauce. Yum.

"That's just it," I replied, pouring myself some Vino Verde from the open bottle on the small central island then heading back to my stool. "Sparkle Toes wasn't too clear. Just burst in all a flutter saying she'd dropped dead in the dressing room at Enrico's, right after her first set."

"Dang," John said, dipping a spoon in a pot and tasting it. He nodded and reached for something in the spice rack, shaking more red flakes into the mix.

"Do you think we should go there?" he asked, turning his dark eyes my way.

"To Enrico's? I'm not sure what good it would do, and I really don't feel like going out tonight."

John gave a noncommittal "Hmmm...." in reply. That usually meant he disagreed with me but was going to find a way to make me come around.

I stifled a groan and took another sip of the tart, pale green wine. There were many differences between my partner and I. He's thin and Asian and runs almost every day. He's also an extrovert who spends all day alone. I'm a short, pasty white guy with a soft belly, and an introvert who works with people all day. So, naturally, as soon as my workday is done, I just want to be home with my sweetheart and dogs.

When John is done with work, he wants to be social.

Over the years we've learned to compromise, and

sometimes that means John goes out on his own or with friends and I stay in with Klaus Nomi and Marsha P. Johnson and read a book. It works for us. Mostly.

Except for times like this, when John leapt on an excuse to go to our local nightclub and cabaret.

I felt a cool draft behind me and jerked my head toward the door leading to the dining room. Marsha woofed a greeting.

"Ghost?" John asked.

"I think so." I was still getting used to having Adam around. The dogs loved the resident ghost, but I was still mildly perturbed by him. He'd been quite helpful on a couple of cases, though, and the house had calmed down since we made him a little altar in the living room.

John already had an ancestor altar in the dining room where he put oranges and lit incense. We'd decided Adam needed one, too, and framed an old photo next to the leather hat the dogs had unearthed from the crawlspace behind our closet. Mostly, I just greeted the ghost's photo every morning, enroute to get my coffee.

"Think he wants some beer?" John asked, nudging past me to get to the fridge. Yeah, sometimes we poured him a small glass of beer. Adam just seemed like a beer-drinking kind of guy.

Marsha barked at John, her whole body at attention.

"Shh, Marsha. What are you on about? Can't you see I'm pouring Adam some beer?" John smiled down at Marsha and Klaus who were both standing now, tails wagging as if they were getting a treat.

"No treats for you," I said. "You just ate your dinner."

Marsha barked again and Klaus just grinned, tongue lolling from his mouth.

"Can you stir that while I give Adam his offering?" John asked.

I nodded, sliding off the stool. He gave me a kiss as he exited to the foyer where we'd set up Adam's altar. It seemed like a good spot for it, next to the living room where he could keep an eye on the space where he used to spend so much time.

As I stirred the fragrant mélange John was cooking up, I thought about Princess Sparkle Toes, Poison Penny, and Sebastian. I couldn't see how Sebastian's troubles at the hair salon related to Penny's death, but a suspicion tugged at the base of my skull, trying to make the link.

Marsha whined and Klaus rattled his empty food dish. Always hopeful.

I turned to where the sweet little tan and white face stared up at me.

"Klaus Nomi, you've had plenty of food for such a little dog."

He barked back in reply.

Marsha trotted closer to me and whined again. Interesting. She didn't seem to want food, but she definitely wanted attention.

"What's up, girl? Any ideas about Penny or Sebastian?"

Marsha barked again, looking expectant, as if she was trying to tell me something.

"I wish you could talk sometimes," I said in reply to her sharp bark, then returned to stirring. Marsha P. Johnson was a very smart dog and I always suspected she clocked a lot of what was going on around her. Maybe I needed to get those talking pet buttons.

But what would I put on the board? A murder button?

A suspects button? And did I *really* want Marsha to be able to speak English?

John slid his arms around me from behind. I leaned back, breathing in the smell of him and the comforting feel of home.

"Smells good," I said, gesturing to the pan with the spoon.

"Yeah, looks like it's almost done. You ready to eat?"

"I am."

I handed him the stirring spoon and went to get bowls just as the rice cooker clicked from cook to warm mode. John always had such perfect timing.

"Hey love," I said.

"Yeah?" John fluffed the rice with a paddle.

"Can we just stay home tonight?"

He flashed me a smile. "Of course. As long as we can go out next week."

"Promise."

I needed time to let this all percolate before throwing myself into the fray. There would be time to head to Looking Good, and time for Enrico's, too. Poison Penny wasn't going to get any less dead, and Sebastian's problems?

Well, I wasn't even sure if they were real.

CHAPTER 5
Marsha

KLAUS SNEEZED. All over my back.

"Watch it!" I yipped.

"Sorry! I just… it really stinks in here!"

I paused to lick the offending spot and ignored my friend. I love Klaus, but getting sneezed on is just too much. When I raised my head again, one of the humans in the room was looking at Klaus. She had tanned skin and long dark hair and stood next to a weird chair that looked really comfy, scissors floating in the air a few inches from another person's head.

When she caught me looking at her, she startled, and turned back to snipping small bits of hair off the other person's head.

Clearly, Klaus's sneeze had annoyed her, too.

But I had to agree with Klaus. It did stink in here. Like weird chemicals and strange flowers. And the music was too loud. It was that bouncy stuff that John liked to play when he was cleaning. I found it annoying, but it seems to make humans happy, so I humored him. Besides, as he sometimes liked to remind me, his writing kept me and

Klaus in kibble, so keeping him happy worked in our favor.

Looking up at Garrett, I saw that he had the same pained look on his face that I probably did. Garrett doesn't like strange smells or loud noises, either. He has to cut the tags off his shirts, because he hates itchy textures, too.

I'd never been in a hair salon before. It was different than the dog groomers, but some of the smells were the same. Except here, stinky human perfume competed with the chemical smells. The dog groomers smells better, because it smells like clean dog. Except the one time I was there when an old poodle was getting certain parts squeezed. Not only did she look miserable, but the stench was also enough to make me want to throw up.

Another reason I'm glad to be the most beautiful of dogs. I mean, other dogs sometimes make fun of my short legs, but in my opinion? My legs are long enough to walk and run, my tri-color coat is glossy, and I have beautiful ears and a graceful tail.

I think the other dogs are just jealous.

"You should come back when we're less busy," Sebastian was saying to Garrett. "I mean… I can't exactly talk with…" He waved his dark hands around at the people waiting in chairs near the front windows or sitting in tall chairs that other humans pumped up and down with their feet.

"*Hey!*" Klaus said, bumping my shoulder. "*Those chairs are pretty cool. Think we could get one?*"

"*Don't be ridiculous. How in the world would you even get up there!*"

"*Garrett or John would lift me,*" he said, voice sounding hurt.

I snorted. *"We're not here for chair rides. We need to start investigating."*

Heading toward some metal shelves with stacks of bottles and small fancy-looking boxes, I began to sniff.

"My nose is clogged from all the different smells!" Klaus whined. *"How do I know what we're sniffing for?"*

"Anything that smells like it doesn't belong."

I knew I was right. But Klaus was also right again. This task was a doozy. Usually, I can keep my nose clear and sniff out what I need, but the sheer number of smells bombarding my sniffer was making me confused.

Garrett and Sebastian had lowered their voices, and despite my sharp ears, competing with the music and other human conversations, plus navigating the smells, was too much. I decided to focus on scenting what I could. Hopefully, Garrett would tell John what Sebastian said later. When Klaus and I could hear. Adam, too. The ghost had surprisingly good ideas about what was happening in the world of living humans, and his dog, Lucy, was okay to play with sometimes. I know she made Adam happy, which was the main thing.

When we first met Adam, he was so sad. Finding Lucy's collar conjured up the little beagle's ghost, so now Klaus and I didn't need to worry so much about Adam anymore.

I got to sniffing around the countertops and shelves, ignoring the coos and lowered hands of people wanting attention.

I mean, I know I'm gorgeous, and usually enjoy getting pets from strangers, but Klaus and I had too much work to do.

Making my way from hair cutting station to hair cutting station, I worked my way from front to back, finally meeting up with Klaus near a door covered with a white curtain. I heard low voices back there and there were different smells, too.

Looking over Klaus's fuzzy blond head, I saw that Sebastian and Garrett were still deep in conversation. Good. That meant Garrett wouldn't try to stop us.

"*Follow me,*" I yipped softly.

Klaus whuffed in response, bumbling into my butt before my nose had even touched the curtain.

"*Not that close!*" I barked. Shoving through the sea of white, I entered a hallway with closed doors on either side and sunlight coming from the end.

I nosed my way along. Behind me, Klaus sneezed. All over my fur. Again. Unfortunately, there was no time to stop and snap at him or clean my fur. But he would pay later.

It smelled like fancy candles and a bunch of other, more confusing smells. At the end, where the sunlight streamed into the hallway, a room opened into a small kitchen.

"*Think they have treats?*" Klaus barked softly.

"*What, does this look like Ron's shop?*" I growled. Klaus was truly testing my patience.

Sniffing my way around a round table, two chairs, and a small refrigerator, I stopped dead in my tracks in front of a cabinet. Klaus bumped into me again.

"*Klaus!*" I barked, forgetting to keep my voice down. "*Stop being so annoying!*"

He gave a short whine but retreated a few steps. Finally.

Craning my neck up I saw what looked like a sink. John and Garrett both told us to never look under the sink. Sniffing the edges of the cabinet, I could see why. At least here. There was a chemical smell even worse than the smells out front.

"Klaus? Marsha?"

Uh oh. Garrett must have heard me.

"We're here!" Klaus barked excitedly.

I whirled and glared at him, lifting my lips in a growl. *"Why did you have to say anything? We shouldn't be back here!"*

I swear. Klaus was pure of heart but sometimes I wondered about his intelligence. Like, all the time.

But it was too late. Garrett's small frame already darkened the door, with Sebastian right behind him.

"What are you two doing back here?" Garrett asked. "You know better!"

"It's all right," Sebastian said. But I noticed he looked around, brow crinkled like human faces do when they feel worried. When he saw me in front of the sink cabinet, his dark eyes widened. Uh oh again. "I'm sure they were just looking for treats. Right?"

"Treats!" Klaus barked, wagging his feathery tail.

"I'm sorry, Sebastian. I'll get these two out of your hair. Sorry I couldn't be more help. But if you think of anything else, just let me know."

Garrett clicked his fingers and quickly clipped our leashes on. Dang.

I'd been so close to figuring something out.

I whined, giving one last look toward the cabinet. Then I allowed myself to be dragged down the hallway and back onto Pride Street.

Sebastian was hiding something. But if that was the case, why had he asked Garrett to come to the scene of a possible crime?

CHAPTER 6

Garrett

PRIDE STREET WAS LIVELY as only a late summer day in Portland could be. The Pacific Northwest was such a rainy place that people squeezed in every bit of sunshine they could get. The only times things slowed down were when forest fires raged further inland or up north. Smoke was a deterrent to even the most dedicated sun worshippers.

Luckily, the summer had been clear of fires, and I hoped autumn would be, too. But you never knew. Climate change made things like fires more frequent.

But this evening? The elms provided much needed shade, it wasn't as hot as it could be, and I had a cold mocktail made with muddle raspberries and mint to enjoy.

My gorgeous husband and I sat across a small outdoor table at our favorite sushi place, How We Roll, the dogs crammed, laying half under, half out of the table at our feet. The patio was half full because it was early yet, but Axle's bar across the street was crowded with post-work revelers laughing, kissing, and occasionally waving their arms along to Taylor Swift. I admired Taylor's business acumen, though her music wasn't really my jam. That didn't mean I couldn't appreciate the delight that other people took in singing along.

John followed my gaze and smiled. "Do I need to make you a woven friendship bracelet, my little Swiftie?"

I smiled back and sipped my iced tea. "I'm good, thanks."

He leaned back and lifted his sweating glass of Japanese lager.

It was nice to sit quietly with my love for a while. If you'd asked teenage me what my life would look like, I'm not sure I would have answered this, but it is certainly along the lines of what I'd dreamed of. To be a young trans man in rural Oregon wasn't easy or safe. Everyone just thought I dressed kind of butch and liked to tinker with furniture and paint. Falling in with the theater kids saved me. Sets always needed designing and building, and I was just the person for it.

I also escaped as soon as possible, heading for the nearest city and somehow managing to survive.

"I love you," I said.

"I love you, too," John replied. "But while we wait for our food, why don't you tell me what's going on?"

"Ugh." I sipped some more tea, buying myself time. "I really want to just live my life, you know? Go to work, hang out with you and the dogs…"

"And our ghost," John added. He was trying to make me smile, and it worked. Briefly.

"Yeah. And Adam. But Sebastian really thinks something is wrong at the salon and Sparkle Toes keeps texting me, insisting that Penny did not drop dead on her own."

"A dragon roll, and your nigiri!" said the chipper

server, plopping a long wood tray down between us. "Need anything else?"

"No thanks," John replied. The woman nodded and strode back across the courtyard.

The server must be Saschi's replacement. I missed Saschi, even though they had been a bit of a pain. No one deserved to die that young. At least we'd figured out who their killer was.

Marsha nosed my leg. I looked down at two sets of dark brown, expectant eyes.

"Dang! We forgot to order sashimi for the dogs."

"We can get it next time she comes back," John said. "Klaus. Marsha. Lie down."

Both corgis whined in protest but did as John asked. He was better at that sort of thing than I was. He could put on that deep, butch voice that I never quite managed, even after years on T. That's testosterone, for those of you who are uninitiated.

We got busy with wasabi and soy sauce and the best sushi in the city. Yum. There's nothing quite like fresh yellowtail on a perfectly formed brick of white rice.

"So…" John said. "I still think we should head to Enrico's tonight. I know you hate crowds and noise, but if Princess Sparkle Toes really thinks Poison Penny dropped dead of unnatural causes, don't you think we should check it out?"

I paused, a piece of barbecued eel dangling in the air in front of my mouth. "You. *You* think we should investigate?"

Usually, John tried to dissuade me. At least at first, until things got interesting and tugged on his mystery puzzle loving heart.

John just shrugged and popped a piece of dragon roll in his mouth.

My eyes narrowed. "You just want an excuse to get out of the house. Because you like loud noise and crowds."

He had the good graces to look sheepish as he swallowed his sushi and picked up his lager.

"Feed two birds with one scone, right?"

I smiled. I couldn't help it. My husband, who blew things up and killed people for a living, using the gentlest aphorism possible was just so sweet. He may have a hard, lean body and a sharp, keen mind that makes up terrible things, but his heart? Is kind of a marshmallow.

I heard a clattering of heels behind me. Both dogs staggered to their feet.

"Uh oh," John murmured. "PST incoming."

I smelled her signature rosewater scent right as Marsha gave a sharp bark. Turning in my seat, I saw both dogs began nosing around Princess Sparkle Toes.

Today's outfit was a slim, pink, early 1960s dress with burgundy chunky-heeled sandals. A gold Star of David flashed from the dip in the dress's bodice. Her hair was an updo of brown curls, and… ah. That's why the corgis' tails were wagging. Slung over her arm was her hamster purse, with Mr. Cheeks's beady eyes peering sleepily from the ventilated plastic. Poor hamster. Sparkle Toes didn't seem to care that he was nocturnal and dragged him around all hours of the day and night.

But I guess hamsters can sleep anywhere, and Mr. Cheeks never seemed to mind.

"John! Garrett! You must help me!"

She flapped her hands, rings clicking and bracelets jangling from her skinny white wrists.

I stifled a sigh. I'd really been looking forward to eating

a nice dinner with my partner before being plunged back into Pride Street drama. Just because I wanted to be helpful, didn't mean I didn't need a break sometimes.

"Never a dull moment," John muttered. Luckily, Sparkle Toes didn't notice, as both dogs were yipping at Mr. Cheeks, hopping up and down in excitement at seeing their old friend.

"Klaus, Marsha, hush!" John said.

"Would you like to join us?" I asked. John kicked me beneath the table. I gave him a look. At least if she was seated, the dogs would calm down.

Princess Sparkle Toes darted her head around, looking for I don't know what, and finally grabbed a chair from the empty two-top next to ours, after carefully setting down with Mr. Cheeks' purse beneath her seat. The hamster got along well with the corgis, which I always found strange. But considering the variety of people I was friends with here on Pride Street alone? I guess a hamster befriending a couple of dogs was not so strange.

"Klaus, Marsha, sit!" John said.

They both whined in protest.

"Sit or no sashimi," he said with a stern look.

It was almost funny how quickly their fuzzy butts hit the ground.

"All right." I turned to our distraught friend. "What's got you so upset?"

"Sebastian has been arrested!"

CHAPTER 7

Marsha

"DID YOU HEAR THAT, KLAUS?" I asked. *"The guy who owns that hair place got arrested!"*

"What's that mean?"

I huffed. I swear, sometimes I wish Klaus was a little less sweet and a bit more savvy. I don't exactly know what *savvy* means, but I heard someone in Garrett's shop say that about a human once, and it reminded me of Klaus. Not.

"It means the police took him away!"

"But why?" Klaus yipped. *"He asked for our help!"*

That was a good question, and one I would ponder while I ate some of the delicious salmon slices John set on the ground between us in a special bowl.

"I'm just beside myself!" Princess Sparkle Toes was saying. "I don't know why they would suspect him! And a Black man at the mercy of our constabulary? That cannot be good!"

"What exactly do they suspect him of?" That was John. He knows a lot about crime.

My attention was split between the conversation and

making sure Klaus didn't eat all of the salmon. He kept trying to nose me out of the way by pretending he was just excited.

"*Mine!*" I growled when his tan snout got too close to the final piece.

"*Not fair!*" he barked back.

"*You ate most of it!*" I glared, hoping to intimidate my friend, but the promise of treats makes him stubborn.

"*Did not!*"

"Klaus! Marsha! Hush!" John sounded unhappy, but his voice made Klaus look up. "I swear. You're not getting any sashimi next time."

I took advantage of the distraction and snarfed the last delectable piece of fish. His tan head whipped back toward me as I licked my chops.

"*Stinker,*" Klaus complained.

"*Fuzz Butt,*" I barked back. "*Now, be quiet. We need to listen!*"

Mr. Cheeks giggled from inside the pink plastic purse, whispering "*Fuzz Butt*" over and over. I ignored the hamster. Sure, Klaus and I might seem ridiculous, but that didn't mean I wasn't right.

But then the hamster said my name. I still ignored him, trying to listen the what the humans were saying above us.

"*Marsha!*" Mr. Cheeks squeaked more loudly. I turned. His little nose twitched with excitement. "*Sparkle Toes was saying the police got the man for suspected murder.*"

"*Murder!*" Klaus yipped.

"*Hush!*" I yipped back, cocking my ears to hear what our humans were saying. All of a sudden, I wished I'd gotten into that cupboard under the sink before Garrett pulled us away. There was something there, I just knew it. But how to convince the humans to let us investigate again? Garrett's hair was looking a bit floppy. Could Klaus and I convince him to get it cut? He said he needed a trim…

"I'm not sure what we can do," Garrett was saying.

"You have to help him!" Princess Sparkle Toes wailed.

"What can we do?" Klaus yipped at me.

"We have to get back into that hair salon," I whuffed back. *"Does Sebastian have an animal companion?"*

"I don't think so," Mr. Cheeks squeaked in reply. *"But Sapphire might know."*

Sapphire was a pampered show cat we'd helped out after her human was murdered. She did love to gossip… but she also didn't get out much these days, so I couldn't see where she would get any intel.

"I still don't see how going to the police station is going to help Sebastian," John was saying. "We don't know anything. At least, I don't think we do."

Garrett tapped one foot under that table, barely missing my paw. I scooted out of range.

"We don't. I mean, I checked out Sebastian's shop, but didn't see or hear anything unusual. Even though he insisted things were out of place and off kilter, the shelves all looked tidy to me. I even checked the main supply closet."

"But you did not look under the kitchen sink!" I barked.

Garrett put a hand down to scratch my head. I mean, I like head skritches as much as the next dog, but sometimes I wished humans were smarter about dog language.

"You have to do something!" PST shrieked.

"Sparkle Toes, you're causing a scene," Garrett said softly. He was right. Everyone had turned to stare at our table.

"Of course I'm causing a scene!" she said. I winced.

When her voice gets pitched high like that, it hurts my ears.

"How do you put up with that?" I asked Mr. Cheeks, who had stuffed something in his mouth and was chewing away.

He swallowed. *"I like her. She's always nice to me and takes me out to see interesting things. You know how many rodents like me are stuck indoors in small cages, day in and day out? Let me tell you…"*

"Mr. Cheeks! Not now!" If I didn't head the hamster off, he would drone on and on. Funny, when we'd first met Mr. Cheeks, he didn't talk much, but now? It was hard to shut him up. Even when he should be sleeping.

A pair of brown loafers approached the table. "Is everything all right here?" Aha! The shoes belonged to the owner of How We Roll.

"It is, Aaron," John replied. "Sorry to cause a disturbance. Sparkle Toes here is just upset."

"Of course I am upset! One of my friends is dead and the other one is being questioned by the popo!"

"What?" Aaron asked, pulling up a chair and plopping down. I poked my head out from beneath the table, tired of looking at knees and shoes.

Aaron looks a tiny bit like John, except he has little pockmarks on his face and his hair is silver and black while John's is solid dark brown that mostly looks black if you aren't paying close attention.

"Poison Penny dropped dead in the club, things were going wrong at Sebastian's salon, and now Sebastian has been taken awaaaay!"

"Sheesh," said Klaus. *"I really wish she would stop shrieking."*

Princess Sparkle Toes had a giant yellow hankie and

was waving it in front of her face, acting like she was going to use it to blow her nose or something. She pretended to wipe the corners of her eyes, but the cloth never touched her skin.

She probably didn't want to smear her makeup. I know all about that from watching John when he decides to get dressed up in a dress and heels. He calls it "drag" though I don't understand why. When I drag things into the house, I get in trouble. Maybe that's the difference. John only drags when he's going outside the house.

"Princess Sparkle Toes," Aaron asked, keeping his voice patient, the way people do to me and Klaus sometimes. "I know you're upset, but can you please keep your voice down? People are trying to enjoy their food."

Sparkle Toes gave Aaron a nasty look. It was almost scary.

"Fine. I know when I'm not wanted! Let's go, Mr. Cheeks!"

She snatched up the pink, hard plastic ventilated purse. Mr. Cheeks wasn't prepared to brace himself and bonked his face against the plastic. Poor guy.

"Sparkle Toes..." Garrett shoved his chair back, holding out his hands as if he could stop her. She towered over Garrett and glared.

"No. Aaron said I should leave, and I will. But if you two..." She looked from John to Garrett and back again, ignoring Aaron, who looked resigned. "If you two don't show up at Enrico's tonight? I'll solve this murder myself!"

She flounced off, heels clomping on the pavement. We all watched her.

Aaron sighed. "I didn't want her to leave. I just..."

"We know." John patted his arm.

Aaron stood up. "Do you guys need anything else?"

John and Garrett both shook their heads no. Unbelievable.

"We want more fish!" I barked.

"More fish!" Klaus echoed.

Aaron looked down at us and smiled. "You two are so cute! Wish I could understand what you're saying."

Then he left, too, heading back toward the kitchen.

"We were saying we wanted more fish!" Klaus barked at his slender back.

I sat down with a sigh. Humans. They would never understand.

CHAPTER 8

Garrett

ENRICO'S WAS my worst nightmare.

As a gay man and a trans person, I know I'm supposed to enjoy places like this, but…. not so much.

John, who sits at home alone all day, making things up, brightened as soon as we crossed the threshold into the already slightly steamy nightclub.

Music throbbed as bodies filled the dance floor in front of the small stage. The scent of beer, whiskey, wine, perfume, and sweat formed a lung-filling miasma. Loud voices competed with the thump of drum and bass, shrieking with laughter and the drama of it all. And by it all, I meant our queer community. Even quiet gays like John and me couldn't avoid the drama all the time. Hence being at Enrico's trying to follow a frenetic Princess Sparkle Toes to an empty booth near the back wall.

I adjusted the fancy new rose-gold circle earplugs John had gotten for me because he felt badly about dragging me into places like this. Repeatedly. He thought they might help me navigate loud, frenetic spaces filled with flashing lights and too many people.

It's not that I don't appreciate the clothes, makeup, pageantry, and overall fabulousness of a night out on Pride Street. It's just…

Complete. Sensory. Overload. And that makes me want to run or curl into a ball and hide.

The earplugs—with a ring that rests inside my ear, looking like jewelry attached to a soft squishy base—were actually helping. This was my first night out with them and they definitely cut the worst of the onslaught. Thank the Gods.

The extra help was good, because following Sparkle Toes through a crowd was slow going. In towering, rhinestone-studded burgundy heels, a silver frock, her brown hair piled in curls on top of her head, PST had to stop, exclaiming and air kissing whoever she encountered.

"This is taking forever!" I shouted in John's ear. He grimaced and nodded, then tapped Princess Sparkle Toes on the shoulder, leaning in while gesturing and explaining something. She nodded and went back to shrieking over a muscle-bound man in a tight white T-shirt. And I mean, I-could-see-his-nipple-piercings-through-the-cloth tight.

"Let's go," John said, gently taking my elbow and steering me through the crush toward where an empty booth sat, looking like an island refuge in a sequin-filled storm.

Two minutes later, I was nestled in the curve of red fake leather upholstered to within an inch of its Naugahyde life. I breathed out a sigh of relief. Having a wall at my back and a place to be that was not in the middle of gyrating bodies getting their flirt on was a huge relief.

"I'll get us drinks," John said, leaning across the table to give me a kiss, his lipstick leaving my own lips sticky.

He was in slacks and a lacy button up shirt, having not had time for full drag. Even in sweatpants, he is beautiful, but around a crowd? My sweetheart lights up like a disco ball.

Seeing John in his element gave me a pang. I really should make an effort to go out to more places with him. The new fancy earplugs seemed to be doing their job of cutting back on my sensory overload, so maybe we could start making more plans.

"Garrett." Enrico himself greeted me, sliding into the booth, the heavy rings on his fingers winking in the flashing, colored lights.

"Enrico," I replied, then waited. Clearly the man wanted something, because he barely ever left his office. I only knew who he was because he came into Dandy Lions on occasion.

A handsome man with light brown skin, he had a sweep of dyed dark hair that fanned back from a high forehead lined with deep grooves that made it look like he was either about to scowl, or express surprise. Enrico also had one of those broad mouths that old romance novels used to call "sensuous lips." Rumor had it that he had a boyfriend who was an accountant and another lover who used to be an exotic dancer. More power to the man, though I was at least twenty years younger than he was and barely had the energy for one intimate relationship, let alone two. Let alone run a successful nightclub on top of it all.

He studied me as if expecting me to bark or something. Finally, he looked away, scanning the crowd, making sure everything was copacetic.

"You hear about Penny?" he finally said, eyes flicking toward the empty stage.

"I did. It's terrible."

John was weaving his way toward the booth, three cocktail glasses clutched gracefully in his slender fingers. Three glasses meant that Sparkle Toes would be joining us soon. I had kind of hoped for a break from her excitability.

"Think you can take a look?" Enrico was saying.

Oops. I'd clearly missed a sentence, ogling my husband and worrying about PST.

"A look?" I repeated, feeling like Josephine Baker, the parrot.

"At the dressing room. You know. Do your," he waved a hand in a circle, "thing."

I turned to look him in the eye.

Enrico held my gaze for a moment before ducking his head. Was he embarrassed about something? Feeling shy? Uncertainty was not a quality I would ever attribute to a handsome, older, successful man like Enrico, but I guess we all have our moments, don't we? Life isn't easy for folks in our communities and having one of your performers die while they were at work must have felt strange.

"How well did you know her?" I asked.

Enrico's eyes widened at the shift in subject. I hadn't answered his question but was filled with a sudden urge to know.

"I..." He slumped as if someone had let the air out of his shoulders.

John reached us and slid the drinks onto the table as if he was a professional cocktail server instead of a nerdy writer.

"Hey, Enrico," John said. "Good to see you out here."

"Uh. Yeah! Good to see you, too." Enrico slid from the booth and shook John's hand before turning to me. "Nice chatting with you, Garrett. If you think you can help me out, just have Jerome or Ace ring my office."

"Sure," I said, watching his back transform as he walked away. His shoulders inflated again, broadening as he took on the posture of a man in charge of his domain. As it should be. He did own the place, after all. Was it my imagination, or did his back slaps and handshakes seem a bit false?

"What was that about?" John asked, sliding an arm around me and scooting two of the shimmering pink cocktails closer.

"I'm not sure," I replied, still watching Enrico's retreat. He was at the bar now, talking with Ace, a gorgeous Black, bald-headed cis lesbian with a million piercings. She also happened to be the best bartender in town. They both glanced back at me. Ace gave me a nod. I nodded back.

"Okay. And what was *that*? With Enrico and Ace? What did he want?"

I snuggled closer, relishing John's slender, muscular warmth and the spicy scent of tonight's cologne.

"He wants me to look at the dressing rooms. Investigate Penny's death. But something is off…"

John took a sip of Ace's concoction. "What sort of off?"

I took a sip of my own. Slightly fruity, without being cloying. Perfect.

"Not sure. I just get a sense that he was closer to Penny than he's letting on."

And what might that mean? I didn't know, but after I drank my one delicious cocktail, I was going to find out.

CHAPTER 9
Marsha

GARRETT AND JOHN WERE OUT, leaving us home with the ghosts. That was fine with me. I needed time to think, and Adam was good at thinking. His dog Lucy, not so much, though she was a cute and friendly beagle who kept Klaus occupied when he started to get annoying.

Klaus lay curled up on his bed next to the cold fireplace, Lucy's ghostly form curled at his side. Touching the ghosts too much made me shiver, but Klaus didn't seem to mind.

Adam sat on the comfy stuffed sofa in his leather pants and boots, and his little leather hat. Even though he was fuzzy around the edges and a little gray, the leather gleamed softly in the golden glow of the lamp Garrett had switched on before he left. John seemed happy to be going out, but Garrett had looked around the living room as if he'd much rather stay at home.

I tried to bite Adam's boots once. Who could blame me? They were perfect biting boots made of heavy leather, with thick soles and a hard toe. It was like biting cold, slimy air. Just thinking about it made my tongue curl.

Pacing back and forth on the patterned rug in front of the sofa, I made a circuit from John's favorite overstuffed chair—which we were not allowed on—to Klaus's bed, around the coffee table, edging past Adam's legs, and back to clear space again.

"*What're you doing?*" Klaus asked in his *I'm sleepy* voice.

"*Thinking,*" I replied, though I thought that would be obvious.

::*Do you need help?*:: I felt Adam's voice inside my head. It felt nice, like a rich, warm, blanket.

I looked at the ghost, then let my eyes slide just past him, toward a piece of art on the wall. It was easier to see him if I didn't look directly, which seemed strange. Maybe all ghosts were like that, but how was I to know? Adam and Lucy were the first ghosts I'd ever met.

"*I can't figure out the connection between Sebastian, the hair salon, and the dead performer at Enrico's. Poison Penny.*"

::*Are you sure there's a connection?*:: Adam asked.

I plopped my rear onto the carpet and whined. There's no shame in whining. Sometimes a dog just needs to let it out.

"*I can't prove anything,*" I said. "*Not yet, anyway. If only I could get back to the hair salon and check under that sink...*"

Now it was Adam's turn to stand and pace. His heavy boots were silent as he traversed the space between the back of the couch and the wall to door leading into the dining room. I bet those boots shook the floor when he was alive. John and Garrett take off their shoes when they enter the house. Garrett says it's part of John's culture. And we get our paws wiped all the time. As if a corgi as beautiful as I am could ever have dirty paws.

Well. I guess I did. Sometimes. But mostly I am quite well groomed.

"Well groomed…" I yipped. There was something about that. Well, groomed…

Adam stopped his pacing and crouched down next to me.

::Well groomed? You mean this Sebastian's salon? Or the person who died?::

"I don't know. Both?"

Klaus lifted his head and looked at us with sleepy brown eyes.

"Did Poison Penny get her hair done at Sebastian's salon?" he whoofed.

"I'm not sure," I whoofed back. *"I think Poison Penny might be like John and wear a wig."*

::Drag queens usually do,:: Adam mused. *::At least they did back when I was going to shows.::*

He sounded a little sad about that. So far, it seemed that he couldn't leave the house, though we'd worked on getting him and Lucy into the backyard. But if even we could go to Enrico's, I don't think John and Garrett would bring a ghost.

All this thinking was wearing me out. Yes, I am a highly intelligent dog, but I'm also a corgi of action. I need to *do* something, not sit around in comfort while clues disappeared.

There was a thumping sound on the porch. Klaus was immediately on his feet, nosing aside the heavy curtains, tail swishing from the split in the fabric.

"Intruder!" he barked.

"Are you sure it isn't just a package delivery?" I asked.

::At this time of night?:: Adam asked.

Good point. Packages never arrived this late.

I shoved myself beneath the curtains next to Klaus and plopped my forepaws onto the wood windowsill.

Sure enough, someone was on the porch, black clothing reflecting the flickering orange porch light.

"Intruder!" I barked, as loud as I could. "Go away!"

"Not allowed!" Klaus chimed in. "Our house! Not yours! Not a friend!"

The person startled and tripped, catching themselves on the door frame with a thunk that sounded inside the house.

Then the rattling metal sound was followed by the shush of paper sliding onto wood.

"Stay here! Try to get a look at their face!" I barked at Klaus before racing to the front door. I screeched to a stop before barreling through Adam, who was already in the foyer. My nose slid through his right boot before I stopped all the way. I yipped, then pulled back and sneezed.

Stepping gingerly between the ghost and the shoe rack, I looked down at a white, folded piece of paper under the mail slot.

More thumps sounded from the porch.

Klaus barked from the other room, "They're leaving! That's right, intruder! Go on, you coward! And don't come back!"

I shoved at the paper with my nose, trying to open it.

The ghost and I looked down at a scrawl of black on the white paper as Klaus trotted in, nails clacking, Lucy following silently behind.

"What is it?" Klaus whoofed.

I looked up at Adam. "Can you read it?"

He crouched down again, one hand hovering near the paper as if he'd started to pick it up, but stopped.

::It says 'Xavier has information.'::

"Xavier?" Klaus barked. "Why would he be involved in this?"

Huh. I looked at my fuzzy friend in astonishment. *"That is actually a good question, Klaus."*

A very good question. And it meant a trip to our old snooty friend, Sapphire the show cat. But we'd need to get Garrett and John to take us, somehow.

CHAPTER 10

Adam

IN SOME WAYS, gay culture when I was alive felt so different to the way Garrett and John lived now. First of all, we had a lot more parties and a lot more sex, it seemed like. Oh, it's not that I didn't know monogamous people when I was alive, but in days before the AIDS crisis cut its scythe through the gay community, things were a lot more free. I guess we were emerging from the restrictions of the 1950s and the pitched battles of the '60s and '70s.

Then, during the early days of AIDS activism, everything just felt so much less… settled than the life I observe John and Garrett leading. You never knew when you or your closest friends might end up in a hospital bed or dead on the streets.

That sort of reality either crushes a person's spirit, or makes one grasp life with both hands.

Also, my friends and I in ACT UP were too busy fighting the world outside to take our anger out on each other, let alone commit murder. Not that gay people are any less prone to violence than any other group. We were just already fighting for our lives, weren't we?

Of course, I hear the current news when John and Garrett talk over breakfast, and it sounds as if things might be getting worse for folks like us again.

And this note that got shoved through the door? And the dead drag performer? None of it sounded good. I'd seen Xavier around a few times. A charming, handsome, younger Black man with a kind face, I couldn't see how he could be suspected of any foul play.

But then, I never expected my friends and I to all die of diseases caught after being infected with a weird immune deficiency because our government didn't care enough about a bunch of queers to bother much.

Instead, they just let us die. Which is how I ended up getting arrested repeatedly, trying to agitate for change.

Until I became too weak to go on.

"What do you think we should do, Adam?" Marsha barked.

Right. The here and now. Not the past.

I sat down on the couch across from the cold fireplace and rubbed my hands down my jeans. I couldn't much feel things anymore, but just that small action comforted me somehow. Lucy jumped up beside me, putting her little paws on my leg, looking up at me with those soulful beagle eyes.

I patted her head absently, thinking, as Marsha and Klaus waited expectantly.

::I can't fathom Xavier hurting anyone,:: I said, *::but that doesn't mean he doesn't know something. You should try to get Garrett or John to visit him. Or they might do that on their own, if you show them the note.::*

Or I could prod Garrett. Since he'd started wearing my old ring, I'd been able to communicate with him a little, which was odd, but after being in some sort of back-of-the-closet limbo for years before the corgis found my box of stuff and brought me back to this weird half-life, it was nice being able to talk to a human at all.

::*We need to come up with a plan,*:: I said, stroking Lucy's side as she settled herself more deeply. ::*Xavier must have some connection to the case that he's just not aware of yet. Or he's not telling. Try to see what you can find out from the cat.*::

CHAPTER 11

Garrett

I WAS ALREADY EXHAUSTED, and the night was far from over. A dressing room used by a rotating roster of drag queens was not the place for a person already experiencing sensory overload. There were no magic earplugs for my eyes, or my nose, for that matter.

Orange feather boas competed with blue sequins and silver platform boots. Wigs of every color—and I do mean *every* color—stood sentinel on fake heads set on shelves above mirrors lit to reflect the layers of makeup required to make sometimes surprisingly masculine people into Goddesses of the Stage.

The show had officially begun by the time Enrico led me into the lion's den, which meant Taylor Swift, Lizzo, and Beyoncé warbled, song after song, above the sound of queens sniping for space as they dressed and leaned into the mirrors, painting on elaborate eyeshadow in almost as many colors as the wigs.

Walking through a cloud of noxious hairspray, I tried to hold my breath, but it was impossible. Enrico really needed to do something about the ventilation back here. I had no idea how the performers weren't all driven batty from the fumes.

"Where are my control top pantyhose?"

"No one wants your raggedy ass hose."

"Here they are, sweetheart!" called another queen.

The whole back and forth was so rapid fire I couldn't really keep track of who had just said what. I turned to Enrico, who calmly leaned against a space of empty wall next to a bank of bright green lockers.

"Is it always this chaotic?"

He looked around the room, which felt claustrophobic to me, despite being the size of our living room and dining room combined.

"Usually its worse."

I groaned, closed my eyes, and inhaled deeply. And immediately began to cough. Hairspray and Poison were a deadly combination.

Wait.

"Did Poison Penny wear perfume?" I asked no one in particular.

"Of course, my pale little dumpling!" said a gorgeous queen with dark skin, red lips, and red eyelashes that spread out at the edges of her eyes like the wings of a tropical bird. "She wore Poison!"

Of course. "Does anyone else wear it?" I asked.

The queen blotted her lips with a piece of tissue, turning her face this way and that in the blinding mirrors.

"Uh uh. No way would anyone else wear her signature scent!"

Then why was I smelling the unmistakable combination of rose, amber, and spice?

I looked around the dressing room, and there it was, looking like Snow White's poisoned apple...a plum-red colored glass bottle on the far edge of the makeup table, cap off.

I slid past a pair of discarded pumps and in between two queens, one shimmying long, shapely legs into a floor length champagne colored sequined frock, and the other strapping herself into an impressive red leather number that appeared to be more buckles than dress.

A performer stood at the long counter in front of the mirror. Her skin was pale, her makeup a dramatic sweep of black and pale blue shading up to white beneath the sharp arches of drawn on black eyebrows.

A blond bouffant wig in a 1960s style matched the era of the white minidress that skimmed her slender figure. Brown eyes cheated my way in the mirror before she returned to applying lipstick and fussing with her hair.

I stopped in front of the plum-red bottle. The scent was strong enough to let me know that someone had depressed the delicate nozzle quite recently. But who, and why?

Not that they could tell me much about it, but still…

I reached for the glass bottle just as the queen next to me blasted hairspray all over that blond wig.

She may as well have aimed it directly at my face. Eyes stinging, lungs heaving, I doubled over, coughing and rubbing at my watering eyes.

"Sorry about that, sweetheart. Gotta be careful in these dressing rooms," she said. "Real careful."

Eyes stinging, throat constricting, I heard her stride off, heels clacking on the floor. By the time I stood up, she was gone.

Had it been an accident? Or had she sprayed my face on purpose? Gah! I really needed to get home, take a shower, and lie down in a dark, quiet, room, cuddled up with Klaus and Marsha.

All of a sudden, I wished the dogs were here, despite the mayhem they would cause in a dressing room like this. Between feather boas, leather, and dropped shoes, there were too many potential toys in the space. But their keen noses would come up with something in here, I was sure.

Speaking of which, now that Sebastian was home—we'd gotten word that he'd been released for lack of any evidence pointing to his guilt—I would need to bring both dogs back to Looking Good. Marsha had been very reluctant to leave the other day, and now that I'd had some time to think about it, I doubted she was just being stubborn. At least, not without good reason.

Maybe Enrico would let the dogs back here during daylight hours when the club was closed.

I mopped at my face with a handkerchief, the scent of Poison replaced by the acrid residue of hairspray in my nose, blinking, trying to clear my eyes. No one seemed to notice, too busy prepping for their time on stage, or shucking costumes by the tall lockers that lined the walls.

After what I hoped was one final cough, I decided I'd better get back to work.

My eyes scanned the surfaces of the dressing room again, looking for... anything. My fingers itched to search the lockers but knew there was no way I'd get permission for that. Not yet, at least. If things escalated, Enrico might decide that getting to the bottom of this was more important than a performer's privacy. Always a hard line, that.

I certainly wouldn't want anyone pawing through my belongings.

The frantic clicking of heels followed by the clomp of

platform shoes caused Enrico's head to jerk toward the hallway leading to the stage.

A Latine queen wearing a turquoise wig and a silver, floor length frock with matching heels lurched to a stop, causing a second queen to almost barrel into her.

"Enrico! Come quick! Jerome just collapsed behind the bar!"

"What in my sainted aunt's name is going on?" Enrico cried out, following the two performers out of the room. The two performers who'd been getting ready followed suit, one of them wrapping a blood red robe around her skinny hips.

"Don't touch anything!" she called out over her shoulder.

I didn't reply, just grabbed a paper towel from a dispenser on the wall and began carefully moving things around on the long counter and lifting discarded garments from the chairs.

There was a matchbook from Axle's Bar, which I slipped into my pocket. Nothing else.

Stepping back, I peered beyond the chair legs to the shadowed recesses beneath the makeup counter.

There. A distinctive white and lavender bottle, like the kind Sebastian had at Looking Good. Crouching down, I used the paper towel to pick it up, hoping against hope it was just a specialty conditioner or something.

It was. I breathed a sigh of relief. But when I inhaled again, an acrid, chemical scent singed my nostrils, making my tongue curl in disgust.

No conditioner in the world should smell that way. This was evidence. Of what kind, I wasn't sure. Now I just needed to figure out how to get it out of here without anyone noticing.

A wadded up fast food bag perched at the top of a mostly full garbage can. Good enough.

I smoothed out the greasy bag and plonked the bottle inside. Then, with one last look around, I headed toward the bar.

Classic Gwen Stefani belted from the loudspeakers and a sad looking performer lip synched along from the stage, blond wig tossing and ripped jeans swiveling.

No one was watching her, though. Every head in the club was turned toward the bar.

Shoving my way through the crowd, I caught sight of John's dark hair, bent toward Enrico's salt and pepper behind the long sweep of polished wood.

When my love caught sight of me, his face brightened with relief. He motioned me toward the end of the bar and flipped up the counter so I could enter.

"Thank the Gods you're safe," he said, giving me a quick hug.

"What's going on?" I asked.

Ace stood, slim shoulders shaking, hands over her eyes. Wow. It must be bad if a butch woman like Ace was crying.

John grimaced.

"Jerome was in the middle of building me another drink when sweat broke out on his face, he vomited in the trashcan, and then collapsed. I climbed over the bar to help Ace, but there was nothing to be done."

"Is he dead?" I asked, stomach icy with dread.

John puffed out an exhalation through pursed lips. "No, thank goodness! But his pulse is thready and it's not looking good. The paramedics are on the way."

Stepping carefully around smashed glass, I scanned behind the bar the way I'd scanned the dressing room. The rows of bottles looked as they always did, reflecting the club lights and being reflected in the antiqued mirror behind the bar, in turn.

The prepped lime and lemon wedges were slightly askew, but the bins of olives and napkin stacks were tidy, and wood swizzle sticks stood proudly in a bar glass as usual.

But it was a lot darker here than under the makeup lighting of the dressing room, making it impossible to see what might be out of place.

The bottle of fake conditioner felt as heavy as my heart. I was exhausted.

"As soon as the paramedics get here," I said, "I want to go home."

John pulled me close, tucking me under one arm against his side.

He smelled of spilled whiskey, spicy cologne, and himself.

But it wasn't enough to assuage the mounting fear that someone was targeting our community.

Now I just had to find out who. And why.

CHAPTER 12

Marsha

"THEY'RE HOME!" Klaus barked.

Sure enough, the familiar treads of John and Garrett's shoes sounded on the front porch, along with the quiet murmur of their voices.

I left Adam in the living room staring down at the sheet of paper with its mysterious message. Between the two of us, we'd managed to get the paper onto the coffee table in front of the fireplace with minimal tears. Adam can't move much in the physical world, but paper was easier than most things.

Speaking of the note, I couldn't figure out what Xavier had to do with anything. We hadn't seen him much—or his uncle, Charles—since just after the big cat show where Sapphire had been cat-napped. After the former self-styled Mayor of Pride Street, Sweetheart Digs, had been taken to a human jail.

Sweetheart Digs was always the center of attention, as self-important as a show cat. I didn't like that at all. If anyone should be the center of attention, it was me. He was a flashy dresser and one of those human men that people either hated or loved. Garrett and John never much liked him, which only cemented my opinion of the human.

As far as I knew, Sweetheart Digs was still behind bars. Human jail is different and much less pleasant than the dog crate Klaus and I used to get shoved into when we were puppies. Thank goodness that phase had passed once we'd proven we were potty trained. As if we would ever think of peeing in the house.

Well, there was one time when Klaus couldn't hold it, but that was before John wised up and installed the dog door to the backyard.

At any rate, I liked Xavier and Charles and, while I didn't always like Sapphire, she seemed much nicer now that she wasn't a spoiled show cat owned by a high-drama flower shop owner. Xavier had calmed her down, I think.

By the time I got to the front door, Klaus was dancing around John and Garrett's feet.

"Hey, you two! What's all the excitement about?" John asked as he toed off his shiny shoes. Garrett was plopped on the little bench in the tiny foyer, unlacing his own shoes. The space was very crowded, but if I waited until Garrett and John were done here, they'd be herding us up the stairs to bed.

"Come see!" Klaus yipped. *"Come see!"*

I nipped at Garrett's trouser leg and barked. *"There's a note!"*

"Calm down, Marsha P! We've already had a long night and don't need any foolishness," Garrett said, swiping at his trouser leg with an injured look on his face. Sigh. I'd been careful not to pierce the fabric. I hadn't even left any drool. Unlike Klaus, who left drool everywhere. Disgusting.

I hoped a long night meant more clues, but there

would be time to find that out later. I ran to the living room, then back again. *"Come on!"*

Adam stood near the fireplace, smiling at us all. He must miss his old family. Lucy was nowhere to be seen, which was odd. Maybe the ghost beagle wasn't used to all the excitement yet. I mean, our house is usually pretty quiet, unless Klaus and I are in a quarrel.

"Okay," John said. "We're coming. Hold your horses."

"We don't have any horses!" Klaus barked.

"We have a note!" I added, for clarification. Humans say really strange things sometimes and we dogs have to keep them on track.

"A note! A note!" said Klaus, bouncing up and down on his front paws.

We finally got Garrett and John into the living room. I nudged the note closer to the center of the coffee table with my nose, then sat back, panting in expectation, looking from Garrett, to John, and back again.

Klaus parked his rump next to me and yipped.

"Marsha?" Garrett asked. "Where did you get this?"

John plunked onto the couch and leaned toward the note. "Well, there are a couple of tooth marks here, and it's slightly crumpled, but otherwise unscathed. Maybe it came through the mail slot?"

"Yes!" I said. *"It did!"*

"Mail slot!" Klaus barked, jumping up and down.

Garrett crouched down next to me and peered down at the paper, forehead furrowed, and mouth turned down. "It says something about Xavier. That's weird. What in the world does he have to do with this? I mean, I know he's bi, but not really a club goer…"

"Too busy with school," John replied. "But maybe he gets his hair cut at Looking Good? I mean, how many hair salons in Portland have any understanding of Black hair texture?"

"Good point," Garrett replied. He stood and sighed, almost backing into Adam, who scooted out of the way.

A quick, muffled sound came from the entry way. Both Klaus and I swiveled our heads.

"What is it?" Garrett asked.

The sound came again.

"I think it's Lucy!" Klaus yipped, and scurried back toward the front door, toenails clacking when he left the carpet for hard wood.

I followed. The little ghost beagle was pawing at a greasy looking bag that smelled delicious at first. Like French fries. Yummy. But the closer I got, the more I smelled the strange scent from the hair salon.

It was the same smell I couldn't get to. The one from under the sink.

And Lucy wasn't really pawing *at* the bag, more like pawing *through* the bag. Poor thing. She had less traction in the physical world than Adam did.

Klaus sneezed. Lucy jumped.

"What is it, Lucy?" I asked, shouldering Klaus out of the way.

"Hey!" he protested.

I ignored him. Lucy made space for me by the bag, scootching her ghostly butt toward the front door.

Careful not to touch anything, I sniffed around the bag, then backed away myself. Whatever was beneath the French fry and hamburger smells was vile. And definitely had smelled like whatever was under the hair salon sink.

"Marsha!" Garrett's voice came from behind me. "Get away from that!"

I jumped, knocking my hip into Lucy which felt almost

as bad as passing through Adam's boots. I shook myself all over, trying to get the sensation out of my fur.

"I was investigating!" I said, feeling a little hurt. *"It smells like the salon!"*

"She's probably smelling whatever food was in that bag before you grabbed it," John pointed out, leaning against the big cased opening that led to the living room.

"Am not!" I barked back. *"I'm sniffing for clues!"*

Adam leaned on the opposite side of the same opening, facing the entryway where we dogs were gathered. But he wasn't looking at any of us. Not even Lucy.

I followed his eyes and realized they were trained on the little side table altar that held his hat and picture. All of a sudden, my doggy heart felt sad. I wouldn't like to be dead, I didn't think.

"Klaus," I said softly. *"And Lucy, too…"*

The little beagle looked at me with dark, misty eyes.

"We have to get to the bottom of this, before another human winds up dead."

CHAPTER 13
Garrett

IT WAS STILL HOT. Sweat beaded on my upper lip. The corgis' tongues were both lolling out as they trotted along ahead of me, one black tail and one tan, looking like fluffy flags. The heat didn't stop them from straining at their leashes and greeting every human, cat, and squirrel we passed. And by greeting, I meant alternately begging for head pats, sniffing wildly, and barking their heads off.

Thank goodness I had a cotton tank shirt on beneath my short-sleeved linen button down, otherwise my back would be a river of sweat. As it was, I wished I'd worn shorts instead of my usual chinos. But, despite the love and admiration of a handsome man, my short, pasty white legs were still something I mostly kept to myself.

I kept switching hands to save the circulation in my fingers and give my shoulders a rest from all the excitable tugging. Half a block back, my socks had begun to slip inside my canvas deck shoes, which was another annoyance. Hopefully I wouldn't end up with heel blisters when all was said and done.

We were off to Charles' house to meet up with Xavier. I

hadn't seen him in months and probably should have texted, but John said not to give him a heads up, which didn't quite feel right. Both Charles and his nephew Xavier were gems, and I hated that whoever dropped that note through the door last night had lodged the tiniest sliver of suspicion in my heart.

This neighborhood had a nice mix of trees. Elms, maples, holly, and the occasional plum or cherry tree graced the sidewalks and small yards. The large Douglas firs that were a staple in neighborhoods further out from downtown were around the only species not represented here. Marsha P. looked back at me and gave a happy yip.

"That's right!" I replied. "We're heading to see Xavier and Sapphire!"

Both dogs loved Xavier and Charles and had come to be at least friendly with Sapphire. The fluffy gray cat had mellowed since losing her human and quitting the cat show circuit. Who knew the snooty thing had just been stressed?

Of course, Sapphire's human had been a pretty high-strung personality herself, before she was killed. I'd probably be stressed and snooty myself, living with someone like that.

Soon enough, we were next to the well laid out garden tended by Charles. He was a chill, older Black man who spent his days gardening now that he was retired. Xavier was a student at Portland State University, and super sweet. They'd taken in Sapphire after her human was killed and we rescued the fluffy gray cat from unscrupulous people planning to exploit her at shows.

Some people shouldn't be around animals. Ever.

I was still angry about that whole situation. It had all been so needless, fueled by petty greed.

The garden was in all its late summer glory. John and Xavier had helped Charles install a drip system a few months back, and the garden looked happy for it, despite the heat. Tall sunflowers lined the far boundary line, heads heavy with seeds, and cheerful daisies and red geraniums lined the pathways.

Sometimes I wished we had a garden like this. I mean, John kept our small backyard really nice, but it was nothing like this.

But then, John and I both worked full time. Besides, Klaus and Marsha would likely wreak havoc on a place without even our tiny patch of flower bordered grass.

The corgis yipped happily when Charles appeared on the front porch of the tidy bungalow. The older man had a gray cap of tight curls that framed his round, kind face, he wore loose cotton pants and a T-shirt that skimmed his belly.

I bent and unclipped the leashes, freeing Klaus and Marsha who surged forward, tails waving happily among the flowers.

Xavier followed his uncle out, dressed in a loose white T-shirt and navy shorts, carrying what looked like two tumblers filled with iced tea in his long arms.

"Garrett!" Xavier called. "Long time, man."

Charles was busy greeting the corgis, scratching their heads as Klaus and Marsha danced around his crouching form.

"What brings you here? Got time for some tea?"

I wound up the leashes and nodded. "That sounds great."

While I'd been hoping to talk with Xavier on his own, maybe it was best to have all this out in the open. He ducked back through the door as I mounted the porch steps. The two glasses of tea sweated on a small wood table, flanked by four folding chairs.

"Sit, sit!" Charles said, waving at the chairs. "And feel free to take one of those glasses. Xavier will be back with mine in a minute."

I sat, then squirmed a bit in my chair. Sweat rolled down my neck, and I picked up one of the glass tumblers just to feel something cool. Portland doesn't stay hot for long, but over the last several years, the temperatures had definitely been on an uphill climb.

Xavier was back, another tea in one hand and a bowl of water in the other, just as Charles took his seat.

Xavier flopped in one of the chairs, long limbs dangling. He looked down at the panting dogs. "I tried to convince Sapphire to come say hello, but she wouldn't budge from the AC, pitiful as ours is.

Portland isn't known for central air, especially in an historic bungalow like this one. Once upon a time, it didn't need it. The joys of climate change.

"I don't blame Sapphire one bit," I replied.

We all sat for a moment, sipping tea and staring at the garden.

"So," I finally said. "This is a little awkward but, we got a weird note dropped through the mail slot last night."

Charles raised an eyebrow and Xavier leaned forward, glass held loosely in his hands.

I fished the crumpled paper from my shirt pocket and held it toward Xavier, who quickly sat up, *thunked* the glass on the table, and wiped his hands on his navy shorts.

"Xavier has information?" His voice rose as he read. "Information about what? What is this?"

I shook my head.

"I was hoping you could tell me."

Charles waved his hand, motioning for Xavier to hand the paper over. The older man frowned, then looked up at me.

"I have a feeling there's more to the story than this paper, Garrett. Why don't you tell us what's going on?"

CHAPTER 14
Marsha

KLAUS LAPPED at the water dish, but he was still laying belly down on the wood planks of the porch, so his snout was practically submerged.

"Klaus!" I yipped softly. *"Listen up!"*

"Huh?" he said, lifting his dripping face.

I didn't reply, just tilted my head and cocked my ears, hoping he'd get the message.

"What's happening?" he barked.

I winced. *"Klaus! They're talking about the case! Be quiet!"*

The heat must be getting to his brain or something. Sheesh.

Garrett was explaining about some performer called Poison Penny. The one Princess Sparkle Toes had been squawking about, sounding almost like Ron's parrot, Josephine Baker.

The rumble of voices was comforting, but it was mostly a repeat of things I already knew. I was itching to be doing something, instead of laying around on this hot front porch.

"And after a bunch of trouble at his salon, Sebastian from Looking Good was arrested…"

"That's never good," Charles replied.

"Wait, Sebastian? He cuts my hair sometimes!" Xavier said.

Ice clinked in the glasses above us. I kept listening, but so far, Garrett wasn't talking about anything new.

"This is boorring," Klaus whined.

I snapped at his paws to shut him up, even though I agreed.

"The thing I don't understand," Garrett was saying, "is why the cops didn't search the dressing room at Enrico's. At least, it doesn't seem like they did. I found at least two clues before Jerome collapsed behind the bar. And I have no idea why they suspect Sebastian since it doesn't seem like they had anything to pin on him."

"Wait a minute." Xavier's voice changed pitch, the way humans sometimes do when they're interested or upset. "What kind of clues? Why would searching the dressing room have anything to do with Sebastian? I thought you said there was trouble at the salon."

"There was. Is. But he was arrested under suspicion of Poison Penny's murder. Didn't I say that? I found a bottle of something nasty smelling disguised as conditioner. The same kind the salon sells. It was tucked under the long counter in the dressing room at Enrico's."

"And it smelled like what was under the sink! At the salon!" I yipped.

As usual, the humans didn't pay any attention. They never do.

Klaus didn't seem to be listening at all, his brown eyes tracked a yellow butterfly, flitting flower to flower. I didn't blame him, not really. The humans were getting nowhere fast.

"I think I might know what the note means," Xavier finally said.

I nudged Klaus in his furry blond side. He startled and snapped.

"What's that, son?" Charles asked.

"I saw Sweetheart Digs on the street the other day. Near school. He saw me watching him and scuttled off around the corner, like a bug. That dude is up to something, for sure."

"Isn't Sweetheart Digs in jail?" Klaus asked me, eyes huge.

That's what I thought, too.

"I don't like jails or prisons any more than the next person," Charles was saying, "but I wish that man was far away from here."

Sweetheart Digs was part of the catnapping ring that had terrorized Sapphire, whose flat gray face appeared in the window, almost as if she knew we were talking about her. No one could prove he'd had anything to do with killing her human, though. Maybe that's why he was out of jail.

"What are you saying, Xavier?" Garrett asked.

I panted, taking a long drink of water. I could see why Klaus had practically dunked his whole head in the bowl. This heat was the pits.

"I'm saying that Sweetheart Digs is up to no good. And he was carrying a bag with Looking Good printed on the side."

"We have to warn Sapphire!" I said. I'd leave it to Garrett to ask who might have left us the note.

Klaus leapt up. We both ran to the door, scratching and whining.

"What is up with you two, now?" Garrett groused.

Charles laughed. "Probably just want inside to our wheezy AC."

"That's not it," Xavier said. "They want to visit Sapphire."

He rose and let us in. I practically bumped my nose on Klaus's butt.

"*Move, slowpoke!*"

Klaus slowed down even more. I know he's my friend, but sometimes, I swear, he annoys the heck out of me.

"*What's happening?*" Sapphire meowed, scratching at her collar.

"*Uh,*" Klaus said sheepishly, pawing softly at the wood floor.

"*You might be in danger!*" I barked out.

Sapphire reared back, flat face looking even more squished than usual. I don't know much about cat beauty, but how this one was ever a show cat was beyond me. I mean, Bruiser has a squashed face, too, and he never wins any awards.

"*What do you mean?*" Sapphire yowled, eyes darting around in terror. "*What happened?*"

"*Sweetheart Digs is back in town,*" I barked. "*But your humans have been alerted, and I'm sure they'll both make sure you're safe. Right, Klaus?*"

Klaus just stared.

"*Right, Klaus?*" I barked.

"*Right!*" He practically jumped in the air when he said it.

I could tell from the tension in Sapphire's body that she didn't believe it.

I didn't either, and I was the one who said it first.

CHAPTER 15

Garrett

I CLUTCHED John's hand as we walked the corridor of OHSU, Portland's teaching hospital. Set high up on Marquam Hill, and on the same side the Willamette River from our Pride Street neighborhood, it may as well have been in a different world. We had to take the tram up, which was frankly the nicest part of the trip. OHSU has some of the best views in the city.

This corridor had none of those views, just bright white lights, the hum and beep of machinery, and the mingled smells of industrial cleaner, pee, and who knows what other bodily fluids. The only time I'd been in a hospital for myself was for my top surgery. I tried to never return, because, though I'm happy with the results, and despite how nice the staff, the environment still made my skin crawl.

At least it was cool in here, which was some respite from the baking temperatures outside.

"You okay?" John asked, squeezing my palm.

"Well enough. Thanks, love." I tilted my head toward his shoulder, which, given our height difference, meant I bumped his bicep. "I just want to see Jerome and get the heck out of here."

My eyes scanned the metal tags beside each door, looking for the number we'd gotten from the nurse's station. Names were scrawled on little whiteboards just above the numbers.

"Jerome Bauer," I said. "There he is." I paused, steeling myself to enter the room.

John must have sensed my hesitation, because he entered first, his warm hand still surrounding mine, gently tugging me forward. Inside the room, white lights competed with the golden sunshine beating against the single window. Machines hissed and beeped, and on the bed, head slightly elevated, was Jerome.

He looked smaller, the way people always seem to when they're sick, especially in hospitals. His shoulders looked less broad, and beneath the pale blue blanket, his muscular legs looked thinner. It's as if our human vitality puffs us up somehow, increasing our size. Illness diminishes all that, and the longer an illness continues, the more a person becomes a husk.

Did I mention that I dislike hospitals?

"Hey, Jerome," John said, keeping his voice soft.

Jerome's eyes flickered, then opened, then grew wide, like he was shocked to see us.

"Whudder you doin' here?" His voice was a raspy slur, his breathing labored, as if it took all his strength to say the one sentence.

"You don't remember?" I asked, stepping closer. "We were at Enrico's when you passed out. John was right there."

Jerome's dark eyes narrowed and his paler than usual

forehead creased beneath his bed-rumpled brown hair. He looked from me to John, then gave a slight nod.

"Yeah. Guess I remember. Ace?"

"Ace is fine," I assured him, even though I hadn't seen the other bartender since that night. And did his question mean she hadn't been to visit? That was strange. I mean, not every person is a buddy outside work, but Ace and Jerome always seemed to have genuine rapport behind the bar. I kind of figured Ace would care enough to at least come by.

Maybe she disliked hospitals, like me. Or maybe she was afraid of something. Speaking of afraid, seeing Jerome made me wonder who in the heck had left that note at our house, and what Sweetheart Digs had to do with any of this mess. I also wondered if Sebastian knew Jerome. They probably did, given that we all live or work in our small village-within-a-city, and a modest sized city at that. I mean, Portland, Oregon isn't exactly New York City or LA.

"What are the doctors saying?" John asked, gesturing me toward the seat next to Jerome's bed. I didn't want to sit down in a hospital chair, no matter how often it was sterilized. But deciding it would seem weird not to, I did, the light blue fake leather wheezing softly in complaint as I sat my butt on the edge. I was really glad I wasn't a shorts wearer. John stood next to me, hand on my shoulder.

Jerome gestured to the lidded cup on the side table.

"Water?" I asked, handing over the cup with its bendy straw.

Jerome took a sip, grimacing as if just swallowing was painful.

"Toxins," he rasped. "Some kind of poison. Pumped my stomach."

I leaned forward. "And?"

His brown eyes blinked at me. "Running tox screens. Dunno yet."

I shared a glance with John, one of those *this really isn't good* exchanges.

"How do they think you were poisoned?" I asked. "Was it in something you drank? Ate?"

Jerome looked out the window, but I don't think he saw anything outside. "Must've been my water. I always keep my steel water bottle tucked under the bar counter. I spike it with lemon electrolytes to keep me going. It's pretty much the only thing I drink on duty."

"You didn't taste anything funny? Smell anything?"

He looked back at me. "I've been wracking my brain, trying to remember that. The water may have tasted a little sharp, but I figured I'd just put too much electrolyte powder in the bottle or something. But…"

He drifted off again, eyes closing. Poor guy must have been exhausted.

"But what?" John asked.

Eyes still closed, Jerome's face pinched, as if he was thinking really hard. "But before I collapsed or blacked out or whatever, I smelled something…Thought someone was doing poppers and I needed to page a bouncer."

"That happen a lot?" John again, keeping his voice casual. I was relieved he'd taken over the questioning, as I gripped my hands together hard enough to crack my bones.

Jerome finally opened his eyes again.

"Enough. It's not a big deal. We just escort the person out and tell them not to come back for two weeks. Let them know we'll be keeping an eye out. Poppers aren't the worst drugs around, but Enrico doesn't want anything taking over the club, you know?"

I nodded as if I knew anything about it. I didn't really. Rural Oregon, like many smaller, remote places, tended more toward meth or even heroin. Poppers were big city sex drugs. The only drugs I've ever done are caffeine, sugar, and a little alcohol. I didn't even do pot, despite it practically being the state flower.

Finally, one of the questions rattling around inside me wouldn't be contained anymore.

"Jerome? What's your connection to Sebastian?"

He looked startled, but quickly wiped all expression off his face. "Seen him around on occasion, but that's about it."

A memory crowded back in my mind. Funny, it had been shoved out by Jerome's collapse, but as I worked on the puzzle, it came loose again, rising to the surface.

"How about one of the performers? Skinny, white? Dresses like she's from the 1960s?"

Jerome frowned. "That's Edie. Named after Edie Sedgwick. You know, one of Andy Warhol's people? Look, thanks for coming to check on me, but I'm really tired now."

Okay. I stood from the gross chair, and John and I headed toward the door. But then I stopped and turned.

"Why do you think someone wanted to hurt you?"

He just shrugged.

"And did you know Sweetheart Digs was back in town?"

Jerome's eyes were already closed again, and he didn't respond. But I saw the telltale clenching of his fingers on the light blue cover, and I swear his face grew two shades paler.

CHAPTER 16
Marsha

"I DON'T UNDERSTAND *why we have to go to the people treats store,*" Klaus whined as we trotted along Pride Street.

I'd heard John and Garrett saying it was going to be another hot day, but at least Garrett was taking us for walkies early, so it wasn't too bad outside yet. Besides, the elm and cherry trees shaded the side of the street we were on. I preened a bit every time a patch of sunlight hit my glossy coat. I look my best in the sun, unlike humans like Garrett who just get sweaty and red.

I ignored Klaus, even though I secretly agreed with him. We could be going to Fred's or Bruiser's for proper treats. Instead, Garrett wanted some salty snacks to take to work.

John and Garrett are both so funny. They're always running into Tracy's store—John for Coke and Garrett for chips or popcorn—thinking the other one doesn't know the first thing about it. Humans are so weird about treats. I mean, what is wrong with treats? They're always rationing out our treats, too. I think they should get over it and just let Klaus and I eat what we want. All the time.

Well. Maybe not Klaus. He gets into some disgusting stuff sometimes. I remember when I had to practically bite the scruff of his neck to get him away from some rotting fish...

"At Your Convenience!" Garrett said, as we approached the green awning ahead. That's the name of Tracy's shop. Humans are amused by it for some reason. Just another thing that dogs are not meant to understand, I guess. They never think I'm funny when I'm trying to be and are not very amused when I do something funny, so I guess it's just a species communication issue.

Or humans just aren't smart the way dogs are. Well. Some dogs. I looked at Klaus, racing along, tongue lolling, short legs working hard. He had a wild gleam in his eye that usually meant he was about to do something annoying.

I sped up slightly right as he careened toward me. Luckily, I was quick enough that he bashed his head into my flank instead of tripping my front legs, like he'd planned.

"*Not fair!*" he yelped, stumbling behind me as I snickered.

"*Nice try, fuzz butt.*" You had to get up pretty early to fool me.

"You two!" Garrett said, stopping next to a curvy blue bike rack. "If you want to come in, you'll need to settle down. Otherwise, I'm leaving you out here."

"*In please!*" I barked, stepping toward the door.

"*In! In! In!*" Klaus was bouncing on the sidewalk in excitement.

"*Klaus! You are not helping!*"

Garrett gave us both one of his *better not try anything*

looks, but opened the heavy glass door, letting us trot in ahead of him.

"Hey, Tracy!" Garrett greeted the proprietor, a stocky woman in jeans and a white T-shirt, and…whoa. Today, her short hair was bright blue, which was kind of cool.

"Garrett! Thank the Goddess you're here! I was just about to text you." She looked around, making sure no one was in the little snack-filled store, double checking the big mirror in the back corner, and poking her head down each aisle.

Klaus was sniffing the floor, while I sat next to Garrett, waiting. He hadn't taken our leashes off, so there was nowhere to go, anyway.

"What's wrong?" Garrett asked. He and Tracy were almost the same height, and their skin had the same pale cast that looked a little weird under the shop lights.

"I saw Sweetheart Digs at the post office yesterday! He's out!"

That wasn't new information, so Garrett nodded and I kept quiet.

"*I don't like Sweetheart Digs!*" Klaus yipped.

"That's right, Klaus," Tracy said, bending down to scritch his ears. I bumped her leg, and she scratched me with her other hand. "He's a bad man. I don't like him either."

"I talked to Xavier, you know him, right? He saw Sweetheart Digs, too. Near the PSU campus."

"I guess since they couldn't prove he killed anyone, the catnapping and fraud wasn't enough to keep him long." Tracy scratched her nose, face scrunched in thought. "I mean, as a queer person, I'm no fan of prison, but I'm also not a fan of him nosing around the neighborhood again. He better not think he's coming back as honorary mayor!"

"No way!" Now it was my turn to bark. The honorary Mayor of Pride Street title had been made up by Sweetheart Digs himself, and a bunch of people just went along with it. I never trusted him. The man didn't even like dogs.

Tracy started rearranging packs of gum and mints on the countertop. "Maybe we could ship him to a wilderness somewhere, where no one has to deal with him, or put up with…"

"What do you think he's up to?" Garrett interrupted. "The timing is suspicious. First weird things happening at Looking Good, Poison Penny dying, and now it's looking like Jerome was poisoned."

"Jerome? From Enrico's? Dang. I hadn't heard about that. I don't know what Sweetheart is up to. He had his arms filled with packages when I saw him, getting ready to mail them out.

Mailing packages… that must be some sort of clue, but I wasn't sure what. Most humans didn't mail packages anymore, they just got them delivered to the front porch. John says we don't get many packages delivered because we live in a walkable neighborhood. Which I don't really understand, because you should always be able to go for a nice walk, right? I guess he means a neighborhood with shops, though. For treats.

"What would he be mailing?" Garrett mused. "That seems strange."

"I thought so, too."

This conversation was getting us nowhere. I tugged on the leash, pulling in the direction of the salty snack aisle. Maybe if I reminded Garrett, we could get out of here and get some real treats.

The door opened and a letter carrier with blue shorts on walked in. Klaus started barking his head off.

"Klaus! Stop that!" Garrett admonished, dragging us both away from the counter. "Sorry about that."

The letter person shrugged their shoulders beneath the crisscross mailbag and swiped at their brown hair.

"Used to it. As long as they aren't lunging at me, I'm okay." They crouched down, holding out a hand. "Isn't that right, doggos?"

I sniffed the outstretched hand and gave it a tentative lick. Tasted like sweat. I was rewarded with a head scratch while Klaus sat nearby, growling softly from the back of his throat. His loss. This person was an expert head scratcher.

But head scratches never last long enough. The person stood. "Here's your mail. Looks like the usual, plus a package."

They set a small box on the counter next to a pile of other mail, then headed to the door. "See you tomorrow!"

"Tracy? What's wrong?" Garrett's voice sounded urgent. I nudged Klaus.

"This package. It looks just like the ones Sweetheart Digs was mailing."

CHAPTER 17
Marsha

GARRETT DECIDED he didn't need to be in Dandy Lion's Design and Decor right away, since Yarrow was opening. I liked Yarrow. They were a good person, super cheerful, liked dogs, and helped Garrett. Plus, not going to Garrett's store meant we could visit Fred at Ron's and get some T-R-E-A-T-S.

Really, I knew Garrett didn't need anything from Ron's, he probably just wanted to pass along the gossip from Tracy. Humans say they don't like gossip, but in my experience they do it all the time. They're worse than the starlings and crows that flit and caw among the elms.

Dogs love gossip. But at least we admit it. What's the harm in passing along the news, right? So we headed back down to Bones, Dogs, and Harmony, a store with big glass windows like most places on Pride Street, and filled with all kinds of things for dogs, cats, and birds. Plus music stuff. John loves music. Garrett thinks it's okay. I'm with Garrett.

Yeah, Bones, Dogs, and Harmony is a weird store, but it is filled with the best smells! Almost as good as Bruiser's

Best Beans. Ron sells records, which make the human music I'm talking about, plus animal supplies and treats. When we walked in, the shop wasn't very busy, since it was a human workday, I guess, and Ron and Fred seemed happy to see us.

Josephine Baker though? Not so much. The African Gray parrot was in a tizzy.

"Bad dogs!" She squawked. "No biscuit!"

"Josephine Baker," Ron's voice rumbled in his chest. "Be nice to our friends!"

"*Yeah*," woofed Fred. Fred was a Labrador of few words, but the ones he said were always good.

Ron leaned on the glass countertop, his long brown locs falling over a patterned shirt that had what looked like human skulls on it, with an orange T-shirt underneath. Skulls were a funny look for Ron, considering what a kind person he was. I would expect someone like Sweetheart Digs to wear skulls, but he always looked like a disco ball instead.

"Any news about Jerome? Or any of the rest of it?" he asked Garrett, who was crouched down unhooking our leashes, *finally*. Once released, Klaus and I both ran to Fred to sniff our friend. He sniffed back, tail wagging softly, brushing against a display of dog and cat collars in a variety of colors. There was a blue one that I thought would look nice against my fur.

Greetings made, I was torn. Scope out new treats and toys? Or stick around to investigate?

"Who let the dogs in?" Josephine Baker squawked in rhythm from her perch in the front window, flapping her gray wings.

"Out," Ron said. "You know the lyrics of that song,

Josephine Baker! I swear, I try to teach you musical history but…"

"Squaaaawwwk!" she shrieked in reply.

Ouch. That hurt. Even the humans winced.

"Come here, you," Ron said, rounding the counter to the window and tilting his shoulder. The parrot climbed on and settled into preening Ron's hair.

"Sorry about that. Where were we?"

"You asked about Jerome. I didn't really get anywhere with him," Garrett said. "But I think he knows something. Or he's holding information back. He seemed weird when I asked about Sebastian and Sweetheart Digs."

"But that's not all!" I barked. *"Tell him about the package!"*

Josephine Baker screamed again, and Ron laid a hand on her head. "Stop. That."

"Marsha, stop barking. You're setting off the bird."

I gave Garrett a wounded look. As if. Josephine Baker had started with the yelling in the first place. I was just trying to remind the humans that there was important news!

"They never listen," I grumbled to Fred. Klaus had already gotten bored and was happily sniffing his way up and down the aisles, probably looking for a new toy. The rule was that we each got a toy every time we came to Ron and Fred's. Which meant we didn't get to visit very often. But that was okay, it usually meant we met at Bruiser's, and Jacki and Bex made terrific treats!

"Tracy had news, though," Garrett said, finally setting the small white shipping box on the counter, next to his bag of chips. "She got this while we were at the store."

"What is it?" Ron opened the box with his big fingers, pulling out a necklace that with a pendant that sparkled in the sun streaming in the windows. He held it up, and it flashed as bright as one of Sweetheart Digs' shirts. "Pretty."

"Tracy is convinced it came from Sweetheart Digs. Said she saw him at the post office with a bunch of packages just like it."

Ron peered at the necklace as we all—except for Klaus—looked on. Garrett and I were waiting for him to find the clue. Fred just waited, because he's calm and patient like that.

"Is that…? Is that an O in the middle of those sparkly bits?"

Garrett nodded. I nosed my way closer, craning my neck to look up at the dangling pendant. I couldn't see what Ron was talking about. The dang thing was too far away for me to reach. Besides, even though I can recognize human writing, I can't read a thing.

Fred sidled up beside me. *"Ron got a box like that."* He barked softly, but I heard the message, loud and clear.

What? *"Garrett! Tell Ron he got a box! Where is it, Fred?"*

The black Labrador walked slowly behind the counter, with me at his heels. Even Klaus bounced up.

"What's happening?" he asked, voice muffled by the blue fish toy in his mouth.

I didn't answer, eyes intent on Fred.

"What are they doing back there?" Garrett asked, right when Fred's black nose started rooting through a pile of mail. Papers floated to the floor around us until finally, he had uncovered a small white cardboard box and sat back, panting happily.

"Oh," Ron said, reaching for the box. "Good job, Fred."

He ruffled Fred's ears.

"Guess we better open this."

There was a rustling sound, and a ball of crumpled up

brown paper dropped on the floor, where Klaus snapped it up and ran. Doofus. Not that I wouldn't have done the same, but not when there were more important things going on!

Ron pulled out a silver chain with another dangling pendant. Both humans peered at it, Garrett's small, blond-covered head almost bumping Ron's larger dark one.

"Is that…?" Garrett asked.

"Is it what?" I barked.

"Another letter, I bet," Fred woofed.

"It looks like a P."

An O and a P. The only word I know that contains both of those is the thing Klaus and I are supposed to only do outside, when John or Garrett has a bag on them. They get very cross if they don't have a bag. It only happened once, though. Now they always have a bag in their pocket.

"Pee Pee Pee Pee!" Josephine Baker screeched.

Garrett sighed. "I guess I'd better see if any other letters of the alphabet are at the store. And text John to see if the mail arrived at our house yet."

"And I'll call around a few of the other businesses. See if anyone else got a package. Or knows anything about what the heck this means."

I didn't know what O and P might spell, but at least we had more clues! And somehow, we had to find that rascal, Sweetheart Digs.

CHAPTER 18

Garrett

THE KITCHEN FELT LIKE HOME, and boy, was it good to be home! A breeze had come up so all the windows were open, taking advantage of the airflow. It wasn't cool yet, but it was nice to smell the garden outside, mingled with the sharp ginger of the salad dressing John was whipping up.

He's a good cook, that man of mine. Klaus and Marsha kept scrambling between the kitchen and the dining room, playing some game I couldn't comprehend. I smiled at the two fluffballs with their waving tails and happy grins. Black tricolor and blond and white, their personalities were as different as their coats, but when they were like this? The differences faded away.

Speaking of fading… the thick silver band on the middle finger of my right hand felt warm, and it wasn't because of the late summer evening. It tingled slightly, letting me know that Adam was around. Maybe that's what had the dogs excited and happy. They both seemed to like our resident ghost. As a matter of fact, they were the ones who had discovered him in the first place, literally stumbling into an old box of his things, tucked in the crawlspace behind the walk-in closet of the primary bedroom.

Adam the ghost had been an AIDS activist in the 1980s, before illness and government neglect took his life. Turns out he was quite the local powerhouse. Beloved by activists, the queer leather community, and every old granny in the neighborhood. And now he was ours, somehow, and had a shrine near the front door, where he could watch the comings and goings of the household, the way John's ancestors hung out in the dining room.

Or something. I'm still unclear about how all this ancestor stuff works. All I know is that since I started wearing Adam's ring, he could communicate with me. Not always. Just when things felt urgent. So, the warm tingle on my finger had me on alert. Did the ghost know something about this latest set of mysteries? Or was he just lonely after years of no one to talk with? I got the feeling sometimes that he watched John and I with some sort of affection. And maybe a bit of wistfulness. It must be really strange to be dead.

"Dinner's ready, babe. Want to pour us some sparkling water? And where do you want to eat? Garden, kitchen island, or dining room?"

Even after years together, John still takes my breath away. A handsome man with dark straight hair cut in some fashionable style that never would work on me, he has gorgeous features inherited from his Chinese American parents, a long, lean, runner's body, and eyes that look at me like I'm the best thing ever. What he sees in me, a short, pasty, introverted white trans man from rural Oregon, with a soft belly and an easily overwhelmed and sparkly brain, I still don't know.

But I'm working on it. The more years that pass dividing the here and now from my old relationship with Vyviane, who undermined me at every turn, the more certain I am that I'm as sexy and worthwhile as John insists.

"You choose," I said, getting clear tumblers from the cupboard, pouring water from the bottle we keep in the fridge.

"Kitchen island, it is," he said, leaning across the white quartz slab to give me a soft kiss and a devastating smile.

We settled in on our stools and tucked into the salad with canned trout, sunflower seeds, flowers and lettuces from John's garden, and a bunch of other chopped goodies, plus the delectable ginger sauce.

"So," John finally said, dabbing at his mouth with a napkin. "You said people were getting boxes? From Sweetheart Digs?"

I nodded and finished chewing the mound of raw vegetables in my mouth. John was getting me used to salad, though I'm generally more of a plate of pasta kind of guy.

"Yeah. There was one waiting for me at Dandy Lion's. I got the letter I. Ron texted me and said Bex and Jacki got an N."

Pulling the necklace from the pocket of my chinos, I showed him what I meant.

"O. P. I. N.," John mused, as I took a sip of sparkling water. "Any idea what it means?"

"Not a clue," I replied, spearing a piece of smoked trout. Yum.

Marsha barked, but I ignored her. Then the ring really warmed up. I looked over my shoulder toward the dining room. Sure enough, a vague gray shape of a tall man in leathers leaned against the door frame.

"Adam?" John asked, voice quiet.

I nodded.

"What do you think he wants?"

I didn't respond, just took in a shaky breath and stroked the ring with my left hand, trying to tune in to the leather daddy who waited patiently. This sort of thing doesn't come naturally to me. I've never been into what some people call "that woo stuff." Never had my cards read, never visited a psychic. The only time I was in a magic witchy type shop was when someone got murdered by the proprietor. Which was too bad. She'd seemed nice until that point.

Marsha yipped again, little paws dancing around near the ghost.

"I know, I know. He's trying to tell me something…"

The ghost solidified a bit more, then mimed pressing something down with his right pointer finger. Almost as if…

::Poison.::

The barely-there word echoed in my head. Adam had said poison.

"Poison?" I said out loud, mostly for John's benefit, but also to give me a chance to think. "Yes, Jerome said he was poisoned. Is that what you're asking about? Because I have no idea why anyone would do that to Jerome."

Except that he'd been acting squirrelly when I asked about Sebastian and Sweetheart Digs.

Wait. Sweetheart Digs.

Adam the ghost made that weird pressing gesture with his finger again. It was as if he was spraying…

"The perfume maybe?" I said.

"P. O. I. N.," John said, rearranging the letters. "Could be. Maybe the pendants are an anagram."

Marsha paused and gave one sharp bark, just as Adam faded away.

"I think you're right," I replied, remembering that distinctive scent in the dressing room. A scent that couldn't even be drowned out by clouds of hairspray, chemicals, or the sweat of hard-working performers. "Poison."

But whether it was the perfume or the thing that had felled Jerome, I still didn't know what it meant. Or why Sweetheart Digs would be mailing cryptic necklaces all over Pride Street.

CHAPTER 19

Marsha

I PACED BACK and forth in the living room, whining softly to myself. Adam and Lucy were nowhere to be seen. John was upstairs in his office, his noisy music playing, keys clattering as he worked.

Sun filtered through the sheer curtains. Another hot and sunny day.

We should have been at the shop with Garrett, but he said he needed some "peace and quiet" to "get things done." As if. Klaus and I were always charmingly behaved. Plus, customers loved us! But Garrett had some important new client who needed her living room re-designed, and Garrett needed to concentrate. Humans are so fragile sometimes, I swear. I didn't see why having two adorable corgis in the shop would be a distraction. All we were going to do was sleep in the window anyway.

Just like Klaus was doing now, when he should have been helping me think about the case! Frankly, we should have been out on the streets, sniffing out clues, but instead we were trapped here at home. At least there was air conditioning.

"Klaus!" I barked.

"What?" My furry friend jerked himself awake, a string of slobber hanging from his open mouth. Gross. He blinked his eyes at me in confusion.

"Where is that package Garrett brought home?"

Klaus raised himself up into a sitting position, then stood and shook his tan and white body all over.

"You mean the little box with the necklace?"

"No. The stinky bag he brought from Enrico's."

He tilted his head, ears perked, thinking, then he trotted to the dining room, heading past the table, toward the long dark wood sideboard against the wall where John's ancestor shrine was. Plopping his butt down, he pawed at one of the doors.

"I think I saw Garrett put it in there. And it kind of smells like it! Sniff!"

I came closer, nose raised. Sure enough, that weird chemical smell was faint, but definitely there. It smelled like under Sebastian's salon sink.

Shouldering Klaus aside, I pawed at the tiny gap between the two doors. Nothing budged.

"Let me try! Let me try!" Klaus yipped, jumping up and down on his front paws, right as I felt a cold draft behind me.

I turned. Adam stood in the cased opening leading to the living room, leather gleaming softly, Lucy looking bright-eyed at his boots. Well, as bright-eyed and gleaming as two ghosts can look when they're semi-see-through and slightly gray.

By the time I turned back, Klaus was pawing at the cabinet, whining and banging the doors.

"Stop it," I barked. *"That's not working, and if we scratch the cabinet, there'll be hell to pay."*

Klaus snapped at me over his shoulder but backed away.

"Well, you get it open then!"

Hmmm… I walked back and forth, sniffing and thinking.

Then, grasping the little knob between my teeth, I pulled, jerking the door open and almost falling into Klaus, who scrambled out of my way.

"You did it!" he yipped. *"Just think of all the things we can find now!"*

Klaus was right. But there was no time for that now. I needed to get the stinky package out and see if it gave us any more clues. I really wished Adam could move physical objects better, but he had trouble enough with light things like paper, let alone whatever was in this old bag. So. There was nothing else to be done but grasp the clue by the teeth. Er. My teeth.

::Are you sure you should be in there?:: Adam asked. *::Usually things put behind closed doors are things you shouldn't be getting into.::*

I glared at the ghost and Klaus yipped.

"If I hadn't gone through the tiny door in the back of the big closet, you would still be stuck in a box!"

A grimace crossed the tall ghost's face, but he didn't say anything back.

My furry friend was right. Both Adam and Lucy wouldn't be here now if Klaus hadn't dug his paws where he wasn't supposed to. Now it was my turn.

I squared my shoulders and stared at the crumpled white bag with its strange combination of smells. Then I noticed I still wasn't moving. I was not grasping the thing in my jaws, now, was I?

I really didn't want to touch the thing with my mouth.

The hamburger and French fry smell had faded, and the chemical smell was strong. I might never steal a hamburger or French fry again.

"Klaus, since I got the door open, do you want to help and get this thing out?"

"Oh! Yes! I want to help! Thank you!"

I could get Klaus to do almost anything if I made it sound like a treat.

He leaned into the open sideboard and sneezed, backing up quickly.

"That's terrible!"

It really was. But sometimes a dog has to do what a dog has to do. Or get their friend to do it.

"Try again!" I barked, then listened for John. Sometimes he came downstairs for a snack or a drink of water. But the music was still at the same level, pounding through his office door.

Klaus stepped forward again, screwing up his little face, then lunged. He grabbed the white paper sack in his jaws and pulled hard, flying backwards. I heard something crack but couldn't tell what.

"There!" Klaus said, panting softly.

"Can you get it out of the bag?"

Not fair, I know. But I really didn't feel like touching the thing. That's what friends were for, right? To do the stuff I didn't want to?

"It really smells bad," he whined, but stuck his snoot into the bag anyway, gripping the bottle and pulling it out until it rested on the wood floor next to the dining room rug.

"Yuck! I think the bottle broke!"

The bottle was soft plastic, but the cap would be hard. That must have been the cracking sound I heard. Sure enough, thick white liquid dripped its way across the floor, snaking toward the carpet. Right past Klaus's paws.

"Klaus! Your paws!" I barked frantically, but it was too late. I could see the white liquid on the fur of his toes, and when he backed away, he left little damp paw prints on the floor.

"Oh no!" Klaus frantically started to lick his paws, desperate to clean them.

::*Klaus! Don't!*:: Adam shouted in our heads.

Klaus kept licking, desperate to get the liquid off his fur.

I didn't know what would happen, but I knew I needed to get John. I raced from the dining room to the living room, then scrambled up the stairs, claws gripping the carpet runner, going as fast as my short legs would go. Stopping in the hallway in front of John's office, I set up barking as loud as I could.

"John! John! John! Emergency! John! John! John!"

The door was yanked open, music blasting, a very annoyed looking John staring down at me with his dark eyes, hair standing up in weird spots like he'd been tugging at it.

"Marsha P. Johnson! What in the world?"

"Help! It's Klaus!" I ran toward the stairs, then looked back. John still stood in the doorway. I ran back and nipped at his jeans.

"Marsha!"

I barked again, then raced down the stairs, hoping he would follow. I heard his feet on the stairs behind me, so I ran into the dining room where Klaus had collapsed on the floor, moaning, Adam and Lucy hovering over him.

Careful to avoid any of the nasty liquid, I braved

touching the ghosts, passing through one of Adam's boots until I was next to my friend.

"Klaus! Are you all right?"

"Don't. Feel. So. Good," he moaned. He was panting and drooling, his eyes fluttering closed.

"Oh no! Klaus Nomi!"

John ran to the foyer where I heard the jingle of keys. He was back in an instant, clipping on my leash.

"Stay here!" Then he ran into the kitchen, coming back with a plastic bag. He scooped the bottle into the bag, gently lifted Klaus, then grabbed my leash.

"Come on, Marsha. We've got to get Klaus to emergency care. Now!"

He didn't have to tell me twice. I whined up at my friend, who lay limp in John's light brown arms.

::*Go.*:: Adam said.

I barked at the ghosts, and then we were out the door.

CHAPTER 20

Adam

KLAUS BEING HURT HAD CAUSED a major uproar, as well it should. Not that any of the victims in this case were guilty, but that sweet little tan corgi? Klaus had never hurt anyone in his life. I just knew it.

Times like this, I wished I wasn't trapped inside the house.

When Garrett started wearing my ring, I held out hope that the connection with him would help get me past the walls, but so far, the furthest I could go was the backyard. Sigh. Maybe someday. But for now… What could I actually do?

I wasn't much good at moving objects, mostly only able to shift light things, but with a lot of concentrated effort, between the two of us, Lucy and I could sometimes move something as heavy as a book.

Which reminded me, last time someone in the neighborhood was poisoned, I'd been able to look through John's reference books in his office.

Figuring John would text Garrett when he got to the clinic, the best use of my time was probably research.

::Lucy. Let's see if we can find anything upstairs.::

She raced ahead of me, paws silent on the staircase runner, pausing in front of the open door to John's office, waiting to make certain I was following.

As my boots crested the final riser, she dove through the door and raced around the big desk set smack in the center of a small room. Bookcases lined the walls, with volumes interspersed with photographs, mementos, and small pieces of art.

It all looked so ordinary. So real. And so unlike the life I had left behind it gave me a pang where my heart used to beat.

::Lucky for us that John does his research the old fashioned way.::

Back when I was alive, computers were giant things that filled air-conditioned rooms. Only a few people had home computers by the time I died. And all the things Garrett and John talk about, like email and social media—whatever that is—didn't even exist.

Scanning the shelves for John's poison section, I saw the book on poisonous plants I'd referenced on that one previous case. I wouldn't bother making the effort to get that down.

::What we need is something about chemicals,:: I said to Lucy, who looked up at me with love in her eyes. I swear, dogs are too good. And that made me want to help out Klaus even more.

An empty slot greeted me on the poisons shelf. Hmmm. What had John been looking at?

Turning toward his desk, I saw it: Mysterious Chemicals: A Primer for Authors.

Interesting… he must be working on a book he needed

this for, because he certainly didn't have time to check this before he took Klaus to the clinic!

::Bingo!:: I said to Lucy, who wagged her whole behind with excitement. Then, with every bit of concentration I had, set about opening that book. The answer—or an answer at least—had to be inside. Otherwise, how the heck was I going to help Klaus get better, and help Marsha and Garrett crack this case?

I may be a ghost, but that doesn't mean I hadn't grown invested in this little family.

They and Lucy were my whole world.

CHAPTER 21

Garrett

I DIDN'T THINK I could sweat this much, but the hot day, my anxiety over Klaus—plus the complete lack of air conditioning in the ride-share car I'd called in desperation —made for a sticky situation. As I exited the compact car, I was happy for the staying power of the zero-waste packaging, all-natural, cedar scented deodorant John had turned me onto. For someone who writes such macabre things while listening to metal, my partner has a bit of a hippie granola streak. It's part of his charm.

John's frantic phone call got me here in record time, and Yarrow was minding the store, so all I had to do was find my partner and my dogs and figure out what heck had happened. John only had time and breath to tell me Klaus had gotten into some kind of poison before he hung up.

My glasses slipping down my nose, my heart pounded as I yanked open the glass door at the emergency vet. It was well outside of our little Pride Street village-within-the-city and John had the car, hence the gig economy taxi service. The scent of animal pee and disinfectant assaulted my nose immediately, quickly followed by the electrical hum of the lights, the barking of dogs, and assorted other animal sounds.

Luckily, I was also hit by a blast of air conditioning, which was great, because, despite immediately raising goosebumps on my bare arms, the animal smells would have been unbearable.

Glancing around the waiting room painted with cheerful graphics of dog, bird, and cat outlines, I saw three cat carriers, a rabbit cuddled in a child's lap, a large Alsatian, and one bearded dragon, but no John, Marsha, or Klaus.

As I approached the open glass partition of the reception desk, I tried to wrestle my breathing under control, wishing I had my earplugs in my pocket, but I'd foolishly forgotten them at home this morning before I left for work.

"May I help you?" A handsome, sturdy looking man in soft blue scrubs that contrasted with his dark skin smiled gently at me. Either I looked terrible, or he was used to dealing with stressed people on a regular basis.

"Um... yes! My partner John Tang brought in our corgi?"

His face brightened, then grew serious again. "Oh, Marsha and Klaus! Yes. Marsha is quite the charmer. They're all back with Dr. de Silva right now. Head through that door and go to the second room on your right. If the door is shut, just knock."

"Thanks."

I rushed through the heavy wood door and entered another layer of animal sounds and smells mixed with chemicals. Along with earplugs, I needed a nose plug, too. Gah! Door number two was open, so that was one less hurdle to overcome at least.

But I still wasn't quite prepared for the scene in front of me. There was dear Klaus, his tan and white body spread out on a soft-looking mat upon a steel table, a woman with dark gold skin leaning over him. On a chair next to the table, John clutched Marsha, who was stress panting, covering John's dark T-shirt and jeans with fur.

My love looked up. "You're here!"

I stepped toward him and gave him a quick kiss hello before patting Marsha's head as she nuzzled my hand. She isn't usually the affectionate one of the pair, but my pets seemed to calm her a bit. She stopped panting, at least.

"What's happening?" I asked.

Dr. de Silva looked up, a lock of shining black hair coming loose from her bun. "We just did a gastric lavage to clear Klaus's stomach. He should be fine, though I'll want to keep him on this IV for at least another hour or so. I also sent the bottle your partner brought in to the lab for testing."

She grimaced. "Despite what it said on the bottle, that was certainly not conditioner! I treated Klaus here for poisoning and you'll both need to keep watch over him for a few days. Make sure he drinks plenty of water and feed him activated charcoal to help absorb any poisons left in his system. He'll also need plenty of rest, though I don't think you'll have trouble convincing him of that."

Marsha whined, leaning toward the table as if she could span the distance and sniff her friend.

"I am required to ask, though," said the doctor, "how in the world was there poison left in a place your dogs could get at it?"

My heart sank. "I'm so sorry. The dogs never get into that sideboard. The doors latch very securely, and I honestly didn't think they could get at anything inside!"

The doctor sighed, turning to the small sink set in a counter along the wall. "Well, it happens. And now you know. Your dogs are too inquisitive for their own good."

"Ain't that the truth?" John muttered.

Marsha barked.

Now that the doctor was done with her examination, I stepped toward the gleaming steel table. Klaus looked so small there, his eyes closed, an IV drip attached to his back, just down and to the right of his scruff.

"Hey there, buddy." I kept my voice soft. "Were you investigating? Don't you know you shouldn't eat things that smell nasty like that?"

John cleared his throat. "The bottle cap cracked and leaked. It got onto his paws. I think he was trying to clean them off. Luckily, this one came to get me. Barked her head off until I came downstairs."

He kissed the top of Marsha's head as I gently stroked Klaus's side. Klaus cracked open one eye, sighed, then closed it again.

"You can visit with Klaus for a bit, but then he needs to rest. I wouldn't mind keeping him here overnight for observation, but if one of you is willing to monitor him throughout the night, he can go home in a couple of hours."

John and I shared one of those couple's looks, trying to communicate a decision. Both of us shrugged. I wanted to bring Klaus home, but I also didn't want to put him in any more danger.

"What do you suggest?" I asked, voice hitching in the middle of the sentence.

"I think that Klaus here would rather be at home, and that one—" she gestured toward Marsha "—will be much happier with that situation, too."

Marsha whined again and gave a sharp bark, as if agreeing.

I looked at John, who nodded.

"Okay." I exhaled. "That's what we'll do, then."

Taking care of Klaus took precedence over figuring out all of these interlocking clues. But the trouble was, he was now firmly part of the puzzle, along with Sebastian, Sweetheart Digs, and…

I gasped. "John! We have to tell the hospital!"

"Tell the hospital what? This hospital? The doctor is right here, babe."

I shook my head, raking my fingers through my hair, almost dislodging my glasses. "Not this hospital!" I tucked my glasses firmly back in place. "Jerome's hospital! I wonder if Jerome was poisoned by the same thing!"

"Wait. What?" Dr. da Silva asked. "A human was poisoned, too?"

John and I both just nodded. The doctor frowned. "Where is he? OHSU?"

"Yes," John said.

"Call me with the name of his attending physician. I can send him the results from our labs. Now I need to put a rush on this lab order!" She hurried out the door.

"Call here in two hours!" she called out over her shoulder. "Klaus should be ready by then."

Marsha whined with worry.

"Come on, girl. Let's go see Jerome." I tried to keep my voice reassuring, but I was worried about all this, too.

CHAPTER 22

Marsha

AFTER SAYING I could go see Jerome, Garrett and John tried to drop me off with Yarrow at the store, but I dug my paws in, growling and barking, until they both finally relented. I mean, who was the detective here? Me! That's who. Garrett and John did okay with figuring things out—eventually, and usually after Adam helped—but I was the one who gathered up the clues.

The humans needed me, and I was tired of them not recognizing my brilliance. So, off to see Jerome and his doctors it was.

Trouble was, once John parked the car, we squeezed into the Very Scary tram. It had a funny name and took us up a big hill while it rocked on a wire, which made me bark and get shushed, of all things! No one else had to be quiet. The people around us commented on the terrifying view, and we almost *died*, and then the bad humans at the hospital would not let me in!

After all I had sacrificed to get up to the human hospital! The nerve!

It didn't matter how much I barked at the doors

shushing open and closed all by themselves, or that Garrett told me my barking was making things worse, the person in the dark blue uniform barring the way would not budge. So, Garrett sent John in to see Jerome as he and I paced on the platform outside. Now that I was on solid ground, I had to admit that the view was pretty nice. Maybe the weird tram thing hadn't tried to kill me. I huffed out a sigh, looking at the hills covered in green trees, the wide river down past the buildings and freeway below, and a white peaked mountain in the distance. Garrett said it was a volcano, whatever that is.

I may as well have been at the store with Yarrow, though. They at least gave me head scratches and treats and would *never* ask me to ride a rocking tram thingy. Plus, even though it was cooler up the hill in the deep shadows of this building, the shop was cool inside. I was definitely panting.

Besides, this waiting was taking too long, and I was worried about Klaus! Garrett and I should be investigating. Talking to Sapphire or Fred. Searching Sebastian's stinky salon. Looking for Sweetheart Digs. Anything!

Above me, I heard Garrett sigh, too. Looking up, I saw he was sweating and looking uncomfortable. Good. If I had to suffer, so should he!

"You know what?" Garrett finally said, looking back at the people coming in and out of the shushing glass doors, and tapping a finger against his thigh. "I'm texting John. If he's not done in five minutes, you and I are booking a ride out of here. There's too much we need to do!"

"Yes!" I barked, jumping up and down on my front paws. *"Finally!*

Right when Garrett reached for the phone in his pants pocket, John came power walking out the magic glass doors that swished open to get out of his way. He looked serious as he strode our way.

"I talked with Jerome's nurse and told them to call the vet hospital about the poison report."

"And Jerome?" Garrett asked. We started walking toward the scary, dangling tram car. I really didn't want to get on that thing again. But I also didn't want to be stuck up here, and corgis aren't so good at climbing long flights of steps down giant hills.

"He wouldn't talk to me," John said.

Garrett stopped, which tugged at my leash, so I stopped, too.

"What?"

"Pretended he was sleeping." John shrugged like it was no big deal, but his face looked very serious. He and Garrett just stared at each other, then John turned and kept walking. Back to the hated tram it was.

Why would Jerome pretend to be asleep? I trotted along behind John and Garrett, trying to delay getting on that infernal machine of dangling death, and thinking about this latest piece of the puzzle. When Klaus pretends he's sleeping, it usually means he's done something bad that he doesn't want anyone to find out. Did Jerome do something bad? Was he afraid of being punished?

"We need to talk to Sebastian," Garrett said. His voice was grim.

"*And Sapphire!*" I said. I just knew that cat was involved, but I wasn't sure how yet. I wasn't even sure if she knew. But with Xavier involved… I also wanted to talk with Fred, Ron, and even Bruiser. I needed to be around my friends. To tell them what happened with the poison.

But mostly, I needed Klaus. He was a goofy pain in the butt, but how was I going to run this investigation without him? I never realized how much he helped me, not that I would ever tell him that. And without my best friend, the world didn't feel safe anymore.

"Come on, Marsha!" Garrett said over his shoulder, tugging on my leash.

I sighed and stepped gingerly onto the darn tram and settled on the floor between John and Garrett's feet. Then I screwed my eyes shut and hoped this ride would be over soon.

CHAPTER 23

Garrett

PRIDE STREET WAS busy with people showing off skin, heading toward Axle's bar, How We Roll sushi, and the other restaurants that had been popping up lately, like mushrooms in a Pacific Northwest forest.

Marsha and I had left John at home. He had some work to do and said he'd make dinner after, so I took Marsha and headed over to Looking Good, dodging bicycles, skateboards, and pedestrians. I was hot, sweaty, and cranky and in no mood to deal with anything at all. But I was also too agitated to let whatever this poison thing was go. Just the thought of Klaus lying on that metal table with an IV stuck in him made me feel ill.

I was worried about Klaus, for sure. But more than worried, right now I was angry. Angry at whoever had switched the conditioner for whatever chemical concoction was in that white bottle. A bottle that had some from Looking Good.

So, we were off to confront Sebastian in his lair.

I wasn't the only one cranky with heat and overstimulation. Marsha pulled on her leash and whined when we passed both Bruiser's and Fred's places.

"You're worried about Klaus, aren't you?" She looked up at me with big brown eyes, with that begging look she gets sometimes. Ugh. It was harder to resist today than ever, but we had work to do. "I get that you want to talk to your friends, girl, but we need to see Sebastian and frankly, I want to get this over with."

Marsha yipped at me in her annoyed voice, but she trotted along just ahead of me after that, almost as if she understood.

As we got closer, the music streaming from Axle's was coupled with raucous laughter and intense flirtation, mostly among men, though the patio out front was filled with people of all genders and types. Everyone was feeling good in the summer sun except for Marsha and me. Axle's... something about the bar pinballed around my brain. But what was it?

I snapped my fingers, startling an older white woman in pink pedal pushers. She almost dropped her ice cream and gave me a frosty glare.

"Sorry," I muttered, shuffling along. I'd found a matchbook from Axle's in Enrico's dressing room. Could mean nothing—plenty of people enjoyed Axle's even though I disliked it even more than Enrico's. At least Enrico's had comfy booths to sit in. The inside of Axle's felt like a half-finished auto body shop or something. People who frequented the space were used to crushing against each other in the mostly standing-room-only interior or using the outside patio when the skies weren't dumping the ubiquitous Portland rain.

No thank you. Maybe someday I'd open a genteel speakeasy-type bar, with low lighting, soft music, and clusters of comfortable chairs… In my spare time, of course.

Finally, we reached Looking Good. The front window showed a few people in the salon chairs, stylists snipping and shaping away, or camped out under the bizarre-bullet shaped hair dryers. And… yes. There was Sebastian, wearing a bright white T-shirt that molded itself to his fit torso, and loose, black linen trousers. Though his tightly curled hair was neatly styled, with a perfect fade as usual, there was a grayish cast to his bronze-brown skin. Was it just stress, or something else?

Hopefully I'd find out soon.

"Come on, Marsha. Ready?"

She looked up at me with her big brown eyes, wagged her tail twice, and barked in assent.

"Here goes." I pushed open the glass door and was assaulted by techno music and the smell of lavender competing with peroxide and whatever other chemicals the salon used to bleach and dye people's hair.

Marsha growled, low in her throat. When I looked down, one of her canine teeth was bared, and her little body trembled.

"Shhh. It's okay." I said the words but didn't really believe them. And was she growling at the smells, remembering Klaus getting poisoned? Or was she growling at Sebastian, who looked up at us from behind the check-in counter, his dark eyes looking haunted and a little bit afraid?

Fury filled me, my feet snapping against the black and white floor tiles as I approached the counter, dragging Marsha behind me. She was still growling, her little paws scrabbling at the tiles as I tugged. I had no patience for negotiating with her, not right now.

"You." I said.

His eyes widened.

"We need to talk."

Sebastian nodded, then turned to a thin young man refilling bottles of hair care products. The natural redhead had amazing bone structure, almost delicate. He looked slightly familiar, but I couldn't place him.

"Rex, cover the counter for a few, will you?"

The man kept his head down but nodded and Sebastian jerked his head in a *follow me* gesture, heading toward the back where the washroom and break area were.

A stylist with long black hair gave me a strange look as we passed her chair. I stared back, worry and anger making me bolder than usual. A guilty look crossed her face before she blinked and returned her gaze to the mirror, as if studying the hair of the man in her chair.

Soon enough, we were back in the little breakroom and efficiency kitchen. I unclipped Marsha's leash and she began sniffing the edges of the room, paying special attention to the cabinets and cupboards. The cupboards with their straight pulls, unlike the knobs that it turned out were so perfect for little dogs to tug open.

Oh, Klaus.

"What can I do for you?" Sebastian leaned against the counter near the sink. Okay. So, we weren't going to sit at the little table tucked into the corner. It was just as well. I didn't really feel like staying long.

"I found the conditioner bottle."

Did Sebastian's eyes widen again before his face crinkled in confusion? Was the sweat on his upper lip because the air conditioning didn't work as well back here, or because I'd just made him even more nervous than he'd seemed out front?

"I… I don't understand. What conditioner bottle? One of ours?"

"Yes, one of yours. But Klaus got into it and now he's in the hospital."

No need to mention I'd found it at Enrico's and that Jerome was also in the hospital. Not yet, anyway.

"Klaus?" This time he really did sound confused.

"My corgi!" I snapped out, right as Marsha began whining and pawing at the cupboard beneath the sink. Right next to where Sebastian was leaning.

Sebastian jerked.

"Get away from there!" He bent to shove Marsha away and she snapped at his fingers.

"Hey! Your dog tried to bite me!"

He clutched his fingers to the white T-shirt covering his chest.

"She should have. What's under the counter, Sebastian?"

"Ju-just c-cleaning supplies." He jutted out his chin, planting himself firmly in front of the sink, black sandals nudging Marsha away as she tried to nose her furry head past his linen trousers.

I didn't believe him, but I didn't try to control Marsha, either. If she managed to get the doors open, I was poised to grab her before she got her mouth on anything inside.

"So, the conditioner…" I began.

"Why would conditioner harm your dog? I mean, sure, it's not great to eat a bunch of it but it shouldn't… Did Klaus eat a lot of it?"

Yep. He was definitely sweating now, and it wasn't the temperature in here, because I'd cooled down considerably since coming in from outside, and Marsha wasn't panting anymore. She was growling low again, as if worrying a bone.

"Klaus barely touched it. He was just trying to get it off his paws."

Sebastian shrugged, but a spark of fear lit his eyes.

"It wasn't conditioner, Sebastian, and I think you know that. It wasn't conditioner at all."

He bolted through the door, Marsha barking, hot on his heels. I raced toward the front, as someone else passed me, heading back to the washroom. By the time I got out to the salon, Sebastian was gone, and Marsha was pawing at the front door, trapped inside.

The black-haired stylist walked over to me. "I think you should leave now."

"Don't worry, I will," I replied. "I just left something in the kitchen. Be right back."

I raced back to the breakroom and ripped open the under-sink cabinet. But Sebastian was right. There was nothing there but ordinary cleaning supplies, and they all looked like the biodegradable kind.

So, what the heck had Marsha been after?

CHAPTER 24

Marsha

KLAUS WAS CURLED in his bed next to the empty fireplace. I flopped on the cool wood floor next to him. Propping my chin on the soft rolled edge of the bed, I sniffed. He didn't smell right—a combination of pet hospital, yucky chemicals, and sick corgi—and was clearly exhausted, but at least my friend was home.

Adam leaned against one side of the cased opening between the dining and living rooms, his leather gleaming softly as usual, despite being the tiniest bit see through. I wondered if I would ever get used to that.

Lucy trotted silently between him and Klaus's bed, a worried look on her faded face. She didn't come close enough to touch me, which I was grateful for. I mean, I like the little ghost beagle, but walking through Adam's boots earlier had given me the willies. Whatever those are. I just heard Garrett say it once, and I know the willies when I feel them now.

John and Garrett were talking in the kitchen, getting human and animal snacks ready. Finally, we were having a proper meeting.

Klaus sighed deeply and lifted his head, eyes barely open.

"*You okay?*" My whoof came out more as a whine. I couldn't help myself. My brow was crinkled, too, which brings my tan markings closer together. Not my best look, I'm sure, though I've been told I'm always beautiful.

"*Our friends are coming? Here?*"

"*Yes. But you didn't answer my question.*"

He just sighed again, lowered his head to his front paws, and closed his eyes.

I guess that meant he wasn't okay. I probably wouldn't be, either, if I had just been poisoned.

Excited scrabbling and barking joined by a sharp cat's yowl followed with a hiss came from the front porch, along with human voices and…

Oh no. A loud squawk. Josephine Baker was here. I hoped she kept it down once she came inside. My own head couldn't handle her shrieking right now, and Klaus was certainly in no condition for a piercing racket.

The doorbell rang. Klaus whimpered.

"Coming!" Garrett called out, slippers slapping as he rushed from the kitchen to the little foyer.

Pretty soon the living room was packed with animals and humans, all jockeying for position on the sofa, chairs, ottomans, and floor cushions. Adam and Lucy retreated to the staircase, which was probably good. The ghosts needed to stay out of the way of the living.

"*You'll let me know if you pick up on any clues, right?*" I asked Adam.

The ghost gave me a thumbs up and tipped his black leather cap on a nod. I exhaled. Okay. It was always a relief to have back up. One corgi can only track so much on her own.

::I didn't have time to tell you earlier, but there might be a clue in the book on John's desk,:: the ghost said. *::But I'll pay attention tonight, in case there's something else.::*

Interesting. I wasn't sure how to convince John to look at anything in his office when the living room was full, but maybe before we all went to bed or something. Although Garrett tried to get John to close the door at dinner time and not go back to writing in the evening. That mostly worked, except when John was on what he called a "tight deadline," which Garrett sometimes rolled his eyes at because apparently, deadlines were things that John set for himself.

I don't pretend to understand it. As long as John and Garrett make enough money to pay for this house and our food, what do I care?

Xavier and Charles sat next to each other on the sofa, with Sapphire on Xavier's lap in the middle, and Princess Sparkle Toes and Mr. Cheeks perched on the other end. Sapphire narrowed her eyes at the pink hamster purse, shoulders crouched and bunching, as if she was going into hunting mode.

"Sapphire!" I barked. *"Mr. Cheeks is not a snack! He's a person!"*

The fluffy gray cat glared my way, blinked once, then straightened up, washing her paws as if nothing had happened.

Former show cats. I tell you.

"Bad cat!" squawked Josephine Baker. She and Ron were on a dining room chair that had been dragged next to Sparkle Toes at the end of the couch.

Klaus winced, but even Josephine Baker's voice couldn't get him to open his eyes. I glared at the bird, who clawed her way back and forth on Ron's broad shoulder, nipping at his long, coiled locs every time she got close to his head.

Sapphire scratched at her blue collar, jingling the tags.

"Josephine Baker," Ron said, turning his head. "We talked about this. You can't yell inside people's houses. Do that one more time and I'll tether you in the backyard."

My eyes grew wide at that. A bird tethered in our yard, with the neighborhood cats on the prowl? Ron was so nice! He wouldn't do that to her, would he? He looked pretty serious, though, and Josephine settled down and began to preen.

Then I caught his wink at Jacki, who shook her head with a smile, and set about re-tying the purple scarf around the short coils on her head. Human hair is so interesting! It is much more varied than dog fur, I think. Like, Bex's hair is short and soft and white-blond. Garrett's hair is called blond too, but it's different than Bex's—more yellow—and I don't know how.

Corgis might have different colored fur, but it was pretty much the same texture, at least.

Jacki and Bex sat leaning against each other on a couple of ottomans Garrett had brought home from the store a couple of weeks ago. Most humans don't like sitting on the floor.

"Okay!" Garrett said, once everyone had a drink or snack from the array set out on the table. We animals all had our own small treats, but most of us ate them right away. Except poor Klaus. His treat rested on his bed, in front of his nose. It was sooo tempting, but right as I leaned toward it, John snapped his fingers at me and scowled.

Fine.

"We need to pool any information we have," Garrett said. "John has agreed to take notes. Right, babe?"

John nodded from his chair and set his laptop on his knees.

"What do we know so far?" Princess Sparkle Toes asked. "All I know is that Poison Penny is dead, and all the performers are upset. Plus, Enrico... it seems like something is really wrong with him."

"More than just having a dead performer and an employee in the hospital, you mean?" John asked.

PST tapped her lips with a bright green fingernail but didn't reply.

Sapphire scratched at her collar. Again. Being always groomed within an inch of her life, the cat wasn't usually a scratcher.

I trotted over to her as the humans shared clues I'd already heard.

Squishing my body between the coffee table and Xavier's knees, I looked up at her.

"Sapphire! What's wrong with your collar?"

She was scratching when we visited the other day, too.

"I don't know," she meowed. *"It's just been bothering me lately. Like something is poking at me."*

"What are you two yapping about?" Charles asked. If anyone else had accused me of yapping, I would throw a snit, but I knew Charles didn't mean anything by it. Charles was kind to all animals. Even the stinky ones.

"Sapphire says there's something in her collar!" I barked.

Fred rose and padded over, leaning past Ron's legs and sniffing at Sapphire, who hissed but didn't swipe the old black lab.

"Can't tell," he said. *"But seems off somehow. Kind of lumpy."*

He nosed Ron's leg to get the big man's attention. Ron ruffled Fred's long ears, but Fred just nosed him again. Sometimes with humans you need to do things twice and insist upon it to get their attention.

"What's up, boy? Marsha?"

I pawed at Xavier's leg, then rose up, front paws on his knees, staring right at Sapphire's collar.

She scratched again.

"Something's up with that cat," Bex said around a bite of cheese.

"Something wrong with your collar, Sapphire?" Charles asked.

Xavier ran a finger under the blue leather, then stopped and looked around the room.

"Something is stuck inside."

CHAPTER 25

Garrett

MARSHA WAS SHOVING her snout against Sapphire, yipping with excitement. Sapphire, jerking with each bump of Marsha's nose, looked bewildered instead of pissed off. This was quite an accomplishment since the former show cat was a bit of a priss and usually loathed having dogs all up in her space. Xavier's long fingers worked at undoing the collar, the younger man bent over the cat, whose gray head stuck out near his shoulder.

Squirming to get away, she began yowling piteously as Josephine Baker screeched. I launched myself toward the couch, switching places with Ron as he leapt from his chair, trying to get the parrot away. I reached over Sparkle Toes, who was holding the pink hamster purse aloft, in a desperate attempt to keep Mr. Cheeks out of the mayhem.

"I'll move!" PST said and surged up and away from the action. I plopped down and reached toward Sapphire to help hold her.

"Oh, poor baby!" Jacki said, but when I turned my head, she wasn't talking about Sapphire at all, but was crouched over Klaus's bed, her hands over his big ears.

Oh no.

"John!" I said, voice sharp. He was still in his chair, frowning at the yowling cat, and looked at me, surprised. I jerked my head toward Klaus.

"Oh!" He lurched out of his chair so fast, he almost tripped over the coffee table.

I turned back to Sapphire, hoping John and Jacki had Klaus's situation well in hand.

"Grab Marsha!" Charles snapped. "I've got Sapphire."

The older man was right. I leaned forward and tugged on Marsha's collar, trying to unwedge her from between the coffee table and Xavier's long legs. She dug her paws into the rug, barking at me in frustration.

"Marsha! Come! On!" I slid off the couch, down to her level, which meant *I* was now wedged between the low table and the couch. Collar in one hand, I grabbed at her shoulders with the other, almost bashing my head. That dang coffee table was a menace.

Finally, Marsha's sturdy black body popped out from the tight space, tumbling me onto my backside, with a yelping dog squirming and scrabbling on my lap. I was vaguely aware of John stepping carefully around me, carrying Klaus, bed and all, as I lay panting on the rug, trying to control an agitated corgi.

"Got it!" I heard Xavier crow, as I finally wrestled myself into a semi upright seated position, keeping a firm grip on Marsha, who snapped at my fingers.

"Hey!" I admonished. "No biting!"

Marsha yipped in surprise and, amazingly, settled right down on my lap. I wasn't in the most comfortable position, but figured I should stay put for a bit, now that Marsha had snapped out of her berserker frenzy.

John padded back down the stairs, having left Klaus

somewhere upstairs. He shivered a bit as he reached the bottom. I don't even think he noticed, but I did. If my usually running-hot man was shivering during summer in a crowded living room? It could only mean one thing.

Adam the ghost was around.

"What is it?" Princess Sparkle Toes asked.

"It's a ring," Xavier said, voice filled with wonder. He held it up. "A diamond ring."

"*Mreow?*" Sapphire asked, blinking up at the sparkly bit of jewelry.

I absently petted Marsha as we all stared at the shiny ring. Her weight on my lap was calming, which was good, because after all of this I needed my weighted blanket, bad. Thank goodness John had gotten me a cooling one for summer.

Adam's ring on my right hand warmed and tingled, which was usually a sign the ghost had something to say.

"Marsha," I whispered in one of her ears, which were in full satellite dish mode. Josephine Baker was muttering from the dining room, and Fred's huff of a sigh was punctuated by one of Bruiser's farts.

"I swear," said Princess Sparkle Toes, who was currently standing next to the fireplace in the spot where Klaus's bed had been, "what do you two feed that dog?"

Bex and Jacki ignored her.

"Marsha, where is Adam?" I whispered.

Her nose and eyes pointed to the bottom of the stairs as she gave a sharp bark.

It isn't that I need to know where Adam is when I'm talking with him, it just feels more polite to at least be looking in his general direction, rather than staring at the opposite corner, or something.

::Adam. Do you know something?::

I felt him considering my question. How I could feel that, I can't explain any more than I can explain talking to a ghost in my mind.

::*Did this Poison Penny have a diamond ring? And if she did, where did she get it from?*::

Whoa. I scooted Marsha off my lap and stood, brushing at my chinos, then plopping on the vacated chair next to the couch.

"Does anyone know if Poison Penny had something like that?"

"A diamond ring?" Princess Sparkle Toes' voice rose alarmingly. "How could a queen like her afford a diamond ring? She worked as a paralegal and a drag performer. Neither profession rakes in the big bucks."

PST was certainly right about that. Even though we all lived pretty comfortable lives, no one in this room made diamond ring and large bottle of Poison kind of money.

"Unless she had a wealthy lover," John mused. Leave it to my mystery and thriller writing partner to think of that.

"How film noir," Ron quipped from the dining room entryway.

::*"Follow the money" is usually good advice.*:: Adam said inside my head.

"Does anyone know?" Jacki asked.

Princess Sparkle Toes began pacing, heels clacking on the wood strip of floor that ringed the patterned carpet. I felt for poor Mr. Cheeks, swinging in that pink aerated purse.

I thought of Enrico. Something seemed off about his response to Poison Penny's death. Like, more than he'd lost a valued performer. And what about Jerome? What was he hiding? Add in the return of former self-styled Mayor of Pride Street and Sapphire's catnapper, Sweetheart Digs, and there were all of a sudden too many questions swirling around.

And that was without touching Sebastian, the stylist at his salon who glared at me every time I set foot past the door, and whoever it was who had sprayed that blast of Poison in Enrico's dressing room.

I either had too many suspects or none at all.

"None of this makes sense," I said into the lull. My usually chatterbox group of friends must all be pondering Jacki's question.

Sparkle Toes stopped her pacing and stood, elbows akimbo. Mr. Cheeks looked relieved to no longer be swinging from her arm.

"Poison Penny dated here and there, but lately?" She fell silent again, one orange painted nail tapping at her lips.

"Lately?" Bex asked from her ottoman perch.

"Lately, she'd been secretive about it. And she had new costumes and new streetwear, too. The streetwear was much too butch for the likes of me, of course, but it looked good on Poison."

"Wait," John said. "I never met her outside the club. What was Poison's street name?"

"Henry," PST replied with a shrug. "Henry Templeton the Third. He/him pronouns."

"With that kind of name, you'd think he'd be a lawyer, not a paralegal," Jacki replied. "And you'd also think he had his own money and wouldn't need a rich lover."

Ron stepped all the way back in the room, the gray parrot still riding his broad shoulder.

"A lot of artists and performers choose a less high-impact profession so they can devote more time and attention to their art. It's not that unusual."

Ron was right, but that left me with fewer suspects once again. Because if Poison Penny-slash-Henry Templeton the Third came from money? Maybe she bought her own perfume and diamonds.

"And not everyone with a rich family has money of their own," Bex chimed in.

Jacki snorted. "Yeah. But you can bet they have a good safety net, no matter how much they might like to 'slum it' with more ordinary folks."

"Not necessarily," John interjected. "Not when they're queer. I mean, clearly Poison Penny has being white with a rich family going for her, unlike us, but sometimes being queer has a way to dissolve those family ties."

Argh. My head began aching. This was all too much. Did Poison Penny have money or not? Did she have a wealthy lover, or not?

What did the ring have to do with her death? Who had poisoned Klaus and Jerome? And whom was Jerome protecting, if anyone?

And then I had a different, even more confusing thought.

Maybe the ring in Sapphire's collar didn't belong to Poison Penny at all. After all, ghosts don't know everything, just because they're dead.

CHAPTER 26

Marsha

IT WAS another "Yarrow mind the store" morning, which I knew made Garrett antsy. Even though he trusted Yarrow, he didn't like to be away from the shop for too long, especially if he had clients to make happy. Luckily for us, I guess, this late summer had a lull in design work, so the shop was the only thing Garrett had going on.

I was torn. I really wanted to catch up with Fred and even Bruiser, but Garrett wanted to confront Sebastian before the salon opened. John said he'd meet us at Bruiser's with Klaus in a bit. My furry friend was feeling well enough to come out in the little cart Garrett used to move small pieces of furniture around. Yarrow was going to drop it by the house before they opened Dandy Lion's.

Heading to Sebastian's was exciting, I had to admit. And it wasn't the hot part of the day yet, so walking down the shady side of the street was quite pleasant. I was a clue hunting machine, a corgi on the case.

We were coming up on Bruiser's Best Beans, en-route to the salon, when Garrett made a noise. I looked up at him. He was grimacing and staring at the tables outside

Bruiser's. Talking with Bex, her short blond hair and pale shoulders shining in a patch of sun as she cleared cups from the table was a serious looking Sebastian. Bex didn't look happy.

Bruiser though? He wagged his stub of a tail in greeting, lifting his head instead of getting up to sniff. I don't know if Bruiser is like those humans who look fine but need to conserve their energy, or if he's just a lazy bulldog. Maybe if my face was smushed in so I could barely breathe, I'd be tired all the time, too.

"Hey, Bex. Sebastian, we were just on our way to talk to you!" Garrett was doing that fake-voice thing humans do sometimes, where they pretend nothing is wrong. "Will you be here for a few more minutes?"

"I just sat down." Sebastian gestured to his coffee cup and a delicious looking pastry. Times like this, I wished I was a taller dog. That pastry would be in my mouth so fast...

"See you inside," Bex said, hoisting her tub of dishes. People were supposed to clear their own, but some of them were as lazy as Bruiser.

"Stay here, Marsha P," Garrett said, crouching to tether my leash to one of the metal rings stuck in the side of the café. "I'll be back."

He looked at me and jerked his head toward Sebastian, his meaning clear. *Keep him here.*

"*Treat!*" I barked as he checked the nearby water dish.

"*Treat!*" woofed Bruiser.

"Settle down, you two. When have I ever not gotten treats for you?" Garrett shook his head and walked into the café, with one last look at Sebastian.

"I really want to talk to you, Sebastian."

Sebastian just nodded, his mouth tight.

I posted myself next to the salon owner, then turned back to the white bulldog who was lounging in the sun, as usual. I growled.

"Bruiser, you are taking advantage! You get treats all day long! I never get…"

"That is not true," Bruiser woofed. *"I am on a very strict diet because of my delicate stomach. I hardly get any treats at all."*

I narrowed my eyes at Bruiser, and he farted in response.

Ugh. He was right about the delicate stomach. But at least *treat* was one bark that humans seemed to understand. I guess I should be grateful.

"Have you heard any news yet this morning?" I asked, right when Ron walked up with Fred, Josephine Baker on his shoulder. Today's outfit was a blue short sleeved shirt over a white T-shirt with some kind of writing and a picture of a dragon on it. Fred had a new red collar that looked nice against his black coat.

Fred sniffed at us both, black tail swishing happily as Ron unhooked his leash. Fred doesn't need to be tethered because he is calm, and slow, and kind of old. At least, that's what he told me the first time I complained about the injustice of it all.

"Hey, Sebastian," Ron rumbled. "Garrett talk to you yet?"

"I'm waiting for him now."

Ron nodded, then paused to scratch our heads before disappearing inside. Humans love their coffee almost as much as dogs love our treats. They don't linger long before they have a cup in hand, I've noticed.

"How is Klaus?" Fred asked, easing his old bones down to the concrete, half under the picnic table.

"He seemed better this morning, but not quite up for a full walk. John is bringing him in a cart later."

Sebastian sighed, scrolling on his phone. It made me realize we didn't know yet if he'd gotten a necklace. I'd actually forgotten about the packages until this moment, I'd been so worried about Klaus.

"Do you think Sebastian got a necklace, too? The humans say they don't spell anything yet." Which meant more had to be coming, right?

"That's a smart thought! He probably did," Fred barked softly. *"And if he didn't, that might be another clue to help us find who poisoned Klaus!"*

And maybe killed Poison Penny. But if Sweetheart Digs had mailed the packages, what was the connection with any of this? And how could we remind the humans to ask?

I heard a bark and snapped my head around.

"Klaus!" I barked back.

"Hello, friend!" Fred woofed.

Bruiser lifted his head and grunted as John wheeled Klaus down the sidewalk in a small red, collapsible cart. Klaus panted happily, looking like he was on one of those big floats at the Pride parade that John and Garrett always dressed us up for. All he needed was a tiara.

Though he looked pleased to be outside, I could tell he was tired. Right as I had the thought, his jaws opened in a mouth cracking yawn.

"Hey, guys," John greeted us as he parked the cart between two picnic tables. "You got enough room here? Or should I move you all to the shade?"

"Shade, please!" I lunged toward the sidewalk, stopped short by my leash.

"Hey, Sebastian," John said, his voice a little cool.

Sebastian nodded, but didn't reply.

As John got us settled, my and Klaus's leashes wrapped around one of the tall trees, Fred and Bruiser settled near the little cart, Ron and Garrett walked out, both carrying trays with drinks and treats.

"Hey, babe!" Garrett said, giving John a quick kiss. "We beat you here, so I got you an iced mocha and a coffee cake. Sebastian said he had time to talk."

Ron gave us all our treats, and we settled in to watch. Or I did. I noticed Klaus still seemed out of it. Like, more than just tired. Guess it was up to me. And Fred. Bruiser was no help.

From my position across the sidewalk, I saw the Sebastian check the watch that winked silver against the dark skin of his wrist. His eyes darted from Garrett, to John, to Ron, then to Josephine Baker, who perched, eyes closed, on Ron's shoulder.

"I can't stay much longer." Sebastian squirmed as they all sat down at his table, scooting onto the wood benches. "What did you want to talk about?"

"Ask him about the necklaces!" I barked.

"Why did you run?" Garrett asked.

Klaus was going on and on about wanting more treats. I snapped at him to hush.

"We need to listen!"

Klaus huffed but settled down in his cart.

Sebastian held his head in his hands, fingers raking through the short, tight curls.

"I don't know," he whined, sounding a bit like Klaus. "I just panicked."

John leaned across the table, gesturing with his coffee cake.

"You knew Klaus and Jerome were poisoned. It doesn't look good for you," he said.

Then I saw it. Peeking out from the pocket of his dark jeans. A silver chain.

"Fred!" I yipped as softly as I could.

The black lab jerked his head my way.

"Pocket!"

Fred whuffed, then rose and walked slowly toward the table until he was right next to Sebastian. The humans were so busy talking, they didn't even notice. I just hoped Josephine Baker didn't wake up from her nap, or the jig would be up.

As delicately as a butterfly, Fred opened his mouth and gently grasped the chain, slowly pulling it from Sebastian's jeans right as Sebastian's hand came down, inches from Fred's nose.

Fred jumped back, chain and pendant dangling from his mouth.

CHAPTER 27
Garrett

"FRED?" Ron asked. "Whatcha got there, buddy?"

Sebastian moaned in distress. He didn't even try to grab the necklace, but he was sweating something fierce.

"Shiny!" Josephine Baker squawked.

Shiny indeed. John reached over and gently took the chain from Fred's mouth, patting the dog's head before wiping the drool off on a napkin.

"What letter is it?" I asked.

"Y-you know about this?" Sebastian stuttered. "The necklace?"

"We do," John answered, head bent, examining the pendant.

"And you should have told us."

I looked at Ron, eyebrow raised in question. He shrugged.

"Wasn't in the salon when I called to ask." Then he leveled his eyes at Sebastian. "Or you just didn't want to talk."

"Bad man!" Josephine shrieked.

I heard poor Klaus whine and was glad he sat at least a little distance away from the noisy bird.

"No one here's a bad man, Josephine Baker," Ron replied, reaching up to stroke her feathers. "At least, I don't think so. Why don't you tell us what's going on, man?"

Sebastian held Ron's gaze, some unspoken communication going on. Whether it was some cis man telepathy, or Black person code, or just my faulty ability to read neurotypical people, I wasn't sure. But whatever passed between them seemed to work, because Sebastian scrubbed at his sweaty face with a napkin, sighed, and sat up a little taller on the bench.

"I… don't know where to begin. Let me text my assistant manager and tell them I'll be late."

I sighed and Marsha barked from beneath the tree. When I glanced over, she looked fed up. I knew just how she felt, especially looking at Klaus in his cart. He hadn't gotten much of the poisonous chemicals in his system, but being small, he'd likely be feeling the effects for a few days. And being forced to throw up couldn't have been fun.

"It's another N," John said, holding up the necklace, as if Sebastian hadn't said a word. Or maybe he was giving the hairdresser more time to collect his thoughts. Frankly, I was kind of over giving Sebastian more time than he'd already had. If we hadn't given him the benefit of the doubt, Klaus might have not been poisoned in the first place. Jerome either.

Marsha yipped again, but my brain was working too hard to pay attention.

"N?" I asked. Poison only had one N. Unless…"Poison

Penny. Why would Sweetheart Digs be mailing pendants that spell out Poison Penny's name?"

"Because he was in love with her!" Sebastian burst out. "And I knew it. Sweetheart wanted to marry Penny, but Penny was being cagey about it, especially after Sweetheart Digs went to jail. I think Poison Penny started dating someone else."

"That might have pissed off Sweetheart Digs," Ron speculated.

"But why the necklaces then?" John asked. "This doesn't make any sense."

"You're the mystery writer," I replied, taking a sip of my iced coffee. "Shouldn't you be able to figure this out?"

John gave me a dirty look, which was fair. I should know better than to bait him, but I was so frustrated.

"Sebastian," I asked, setting my coffee down with a *thunk*. "What's the story with the poisoned conditioner? How did it get to Enrico's dressing room? Was someone jealous of Poison Penny?"

And why was Jerome poisoned? That was another thing that confused the heck out of me, especially since the bartender had clammed up.

Sebastian shuddered.

"Just tell us," Ron said softly.

"Here's the thing," Sebastian said. "I'm confused, myself. I mean, I came to you for help, remember?"

He was looking straight at me, eyes pleading.

"That's right. You said someone was trying to sabotage the salon."

"Sabotage how?" Ron asked.

Sebastian looked past Ron, as if the answer could be found in the reflections in the big café window.

"Little things at first. A stylist's combs not being at their station. Someone's best pair of scissors missing. It got so our stylists and nail tech started taking their more expensive tools home every night, which, let me tell you, does not make for the most congenial atmosphere. But I couldn't blame them."

He sighed, a little deflated.

"What else?" John asked. I could almost see him taking notes in his head. He's got quite a brain, that man of mine.

"A couple of people threatened to give up their chair rentals, which would have really hurt business, you know? And then products started to get switched around, in ways that could've caused a minor catastrophe. Stuff like curl activator bottles on the conditioner shelves. Chemicals missing. Cleaning products that should've stayed in the breakroom or janitor closet ending up on the shop floor…"

"Who has keys, besides you?" I asked.

"Me, and my assistant manager, Carly. But it can't be her…"

John snorted, but just took another bite of his coffee cake.

"No, I mean it. I know not everyone is as trustworthy as they seem, but she was out sick for some of the events."

"Out sick doesn't mean she didn't sneak in after hours," Ron pointed out.

Sebastian looked startled, as if he hadn't thought about that. Wow. And I thought I was naive sometimes.

Wait a minute.

"Is this Carly also a stylist?" I asked. "White woman. Long dark hair?"

"Oh. Yeah. I can't afford a full-time manager, and she makes better money as a stylist than I could ever pay. I just supplement her income to cover things when I need a day off or am running late or something. That's why she has the keys."

Well, Carly was heading to the top of my suspect list now, that was for sure.

"Did Carly ever go to Enrico's?" John asked.

Sebastian shrugged. "I mean, she's pansexual, so yeah? I think so?"

Then he snapped his long fingers. "Yes! She does go there sometimes! She mentioned thinking Ace was hot."

"Who's Ace?" Ron asked, brow furrowed.

I barked out a short laugh. "Sometimes I forget you're not one of us."

"Hey, now," Ron replied. "Just because I've only dated women for the last decade, doesn't mean I don't still have my queer side. I just don't like hanging out in clubs much. Give me a concert any day, but crowded clubs where everyone's getting drunk? Not my scene. Besides, I'm demi, and picking up strangers is never going to work for me anyway."

"I stand corrected," I said, tucking that information away. Ron was demisexual and bi or pan romantic? Cool. I should know better than to assume anyone's sexual orientation without asking. I mean, being trans, I did my best to not assume gender, but clearly needed to up my game in the LGBTQIA+ inclusivity Olympics.

"Ace is one of the bartenders at Enrico's. Works with Jerome."

Jerome who was still in the hospital.

"But why do you want to know if Carly goes to Enrico's?" Sebastian asked.

All three of us just looked at him until his face changed as he had his little lightbulb moment.

"You think Carly poisoned Jerome. Do you think she killed Penny, too?"

He sounded so defeated, I wanted to reach out and comfort him. Almost. He may have moved down on the suspect roster, while I bumped Carly to the top, but until we solved this case, Sebastian was still on the list.

CHAPTER 28

Adam

GARRETT FINALLY HAD to go to the shop and work on his client designs, or so he said. He and John both had such interesting jobs, and ones that working class me would never have thought were possible.

At any rate, John decided he wanted Klaus nearby while he worked, so both dog beds and a water bowl had been dragged from the main bedroom to the hallway just outside John's office, where he was currently staring at his computer screen a lot more than his fingers were tapping away.

Guess it's hard to work on a fake mystery when a real mystery was overtaking your life.

I kept hoping John would notice the book he'd left on his desk. The one where I'd found the page about formaldehyde. It was either that, or paraphenylenedi-amine. I'd worked for half an hour to place a bookmark on that page, just in case.

So far, John seemed absorbed in the staring contest with his monitor, rather than his research materials. If I could figure out how to use Marsha to alert him to the book, I would. But the corgi's legs were too short to leap up on John's desk, and besides, I didn't want to risk her knocking the book off the desk and closing the formalde-hyde page.

Guess I'd just hope the handsome man would figure it out on his own. He was certainly smart enough.

Now it was just a frustrating waiting game, with me sitting at the top of the stairs and Lucy at my side as Klaus lay in his bed and Marsha paced up and down the hall-way, padding down the patterned carpet runner of the old historic house.

I'd come to rely on the mysteries the little dogs brought home. Otherwise, being a ghost was kind of boring.

::*You need to get to the bottom of these necklaces and find Sweetheart Digs,*:: I said.

"*But how are we supposed to do that?*" Marsha whined, deep in her throat. She then proceeded to snap her teeth in the air and growl, as if she was biting our old nemesis in the leg.

::*And what about that ring? It looked like an engagement ring of some sort. I really think it belonged to this Poison Penny.*::

"*But who gave it to her?*" Klaus yipped sleepily. He rose just enough to lap at some water, which was good. I'd heard John and Garrett talking about the need to keep the little corgi hydrated.

::*Seems like it has to be Sweetheart Digs, doesn't it? Unless…*::

"*Unless what?*" Marsha barked, as John finally began typing.

::*Unless Enrico has something to do with all of this. One person at his nightclub is dead, and another is in the hospital with poisoning.*::

Marsha gasped.

"*You're right! John!*" she barked "*You and Garrett have to talk to Enrico!*"

The typing stopped and John groaned.

"Marsha P, I just got back to work. Can you be quiet? Just for an hour? I need to finish this chapter."

Marsha whuffed in irritation then trotted down the hall. Klaus and I just looked at each other, waiting.

Soon enough, the corgi came trotting proudly back down the hallway, head held high, tan and white points gleaming like makeup on her little black face. And she carried a pink feather boa in her jaws.

I snorted, and Lucy gave a silent bark.

::That's one way to get a certain type of gender-bending man to a nightclub.::

Too bad I couldn't go along myself.

CHAPTER 29
Marsha

JOHN FINALLY DECIDED he wasn't going to get any more writing done with me and Klaus "bugging him so much." As if two sweet little corgis would ever be a bother to anyone!

At least he'd laughed when I brought the feather boa into the office, and texted Garrett that they should go to Enrico's later. Hopefully, that meant Adam would get his wish and more clues were on their way. But for now? I'd managed to convince John to leave the house, so off we went, with Klaus riding happily behind us in the little cart.

Trouble was, I wasn't sure where we needed to go. At first, I'd thought about leading him to visit Sapphire, but I didn't think the former show cat would have more information this soon after our meeting. Looking at the ring wouldn't help us. We needed to find out where the thing had come from.

So, we strolled down Pride Street, as usual, with John passing all of our usual spots. He didn't even stop by Dandy Lion's to give Garrett a kiss. That could only mean one thing.

John was taking us to Tracy's store to get some human snacks! You'd think both he and Garrett would have figured out they both used the convenience store to get forbidden treats, but they never seemed to catch on.

Or maybe they did and just pretended not to know. Humans are very strange, and in all my years around them, I still hadn't figured some things out. Dogs are a lot more simple. They tell you when they're happy, angry, or afraid. You know if a dog likes you or wishes you were dead. Humans? It seems like they just can't tell who to trust, and who is lying, or even who wants to be friends half the time.

Dogs are much better about sensing what's going on, with other dogs and with humans, too.

I sniffed my way down the sidewalk, pausing occasionally to check on who had already been out and about, and if there were messages to glean.

The distinct whir and whoosh sound of a skateboard pricked up my ears.

"Slow down! There are children and dogs here! If I wasn't on this leash, I'd bite your ankles! That's right! Keep moving, buddy!"

"Marsha P. Johnson," John said. "It's just a skateboard."

Hmph. John did not understand the threat four wheels could pose on doggy toes. And he also didn't understand that sometimes a dog just needs to bark.

"We going to visit Tracy?" Klaus yipped.

I didn't bother turning around, though I slowed a little, falling slightly behind John's long stride.

"Sure seems that way. Maybe she knows more about the necklaces and Sweetheart Digs!" I yipped back.

At least, I hoped so. Adam was right, we really needed

to figure this out. After Klaus got poisoned, and with the weird way Sebastian was acting, I couldn't help but think that someone else might be next.

I shivered a bit, despite the hot day, shaking the chills off my fur before trotting on ahead.

By the time we reached the green awning, I was ready for a treat myself.

John led us in, bumping the cart into the store.

"Tracy?"

She wasn't up at the counter.

"Maybe she's stocking things!" I barked, lunging toward the back aisle. I loved it when Tracy was stocking things. It meant boxes and wrapping to jump on. And sometimes a treat.

"Marsha!" John pulled me up short and unclipped my leash. "I swear. You are out of control today!"

"Am not!" I said, racing around the corner, paws scrabbling for purchase on the smooth floors. Along with fruit punch, some old milk that must've gotten spilled a long time ago, and various potato chip and cookie smells, I caught Tracy's scent. I followed it all the way to the back corner where cleaning supply smells mingled with the weird cool smell of the wall of cold drinks, eggs, and—my favorite—cheese.

Tracy sat slumped against one of the cooler doors where John got his secret Coca Colas. Sure enough, a half-unpacked box was next to her. She must have been re-stocking the cleaning products that faced the cooler wall.

She was crying, tears rolling down her pale cheeks, round belly and chest shaking, and her muscular shoulders caved in defeat.

I gave one sharp bark to let John know where I was

and heard the sound of his feet and Klaus's cart, slowly wheeling our way.

Tracy looked at me and sniffed. I licked her hand, and she gave me a half smile before patting my head.

"Hello, Marsha."

"Tracy, what's wrong? Did something happen?" John asked, parking the cart against another cooler door.

"Jerome died. I just got a call from his brother. Renal failure.

"What?" John said. "I just saw him!"

"What?" I barked.

Klaus looked stunned.

Two humans were dead now. I looked at Klaus's shocked face and couldn't help but feel a pang that, if it weren't for my quick thinking, he might be dead, too.

John grabbed a box of tissues and handed them to Tracy, who nodded, ripped the box open and grabbed a handful, loudly blowing her nose.

"Maybe Jerome wasn't pretending to be sleeping when I was there..." John said, crouching down across from Tracy. "Maybe he was getting worse, instead of better."

"I just can't believe it," Tracy moaned. "Who would do this? And why?"

"Tracy! What about Sweetheart Digs? Have you seen him again?" I whoofed.

"Thanks, Marsha. I appreciate it," Tracy said, petting my back.

"She doesn't understand," Klaus said, softly.

"I know. But we have to make her understand."

But how? I looked around for something that I could use to tell the humans they needed to stop sitting here on the floor and find Sweetheart Digs...

John's ring. I nuzzled his hand, trying to get him to look down, but he just patted my head absently, staring off into space.

Drat!

The door at the front of the shop opened and a voice called back.

"Tracy?"

"It's Xavier!"

"Marsha? Is that you?"

Tracy cleared her throat.

"Back here," she called out, then struggled to her feet, with John helping her.

Xavier came loping back on those long legs of his. He smelled like Xavier, but there was also a different smell. A smell I recognized and didn't like very much.

I sneezed.

"Oh! Hi, John! Hi, Klaus and Marsha! Klaus is feeling better?" he asked John.

"Almost better! But my tummy still hurts." Klaus woofed.

"Getting there," John replied.

"Xavier, why are you here?" Tracy asked. "Don't you have classes right now?"

"I skipped out. I ran into someone who wanted to talk to you."

The sneezy smell grew stronger as footsteps sounded down the center aisle.

And Sweetheart Digs appeared, stinking like patchouli. But where he used to dress in bright, shiny clothes, swaggering around being loud as if he owned the whole street, he looked defeated. Even his flowered shirt seemed rumpled and subdued, and his always fair skin was almost as ghostly as Adam's.

"You," John said, almost growling.

Guess we didn't need to ask Tracy if she'd seen the former Mayor of Pride Street.

"Me," Sweetheart Digs replied. "I'm so sorry. For everything."

And then he burst into tears.

CHAPTER 30

Garrett

"WHAT DO YOU MEAN, Sweetheart Digs is coming here?" Yarrow was rubbing a polishing cloth so hard against a 1920s vanity mirror I thought they might crack it. I never thought their skinny arms had that much muscle, but once again, Yarrow proved me wrong.

They turned, dark brown hands fisted on the hips of their white linen trousers, rainbow platform sneakers peeking out from beneath, matching the rainbow on the black t-shirt that skimmed their torso.

"I cannot believe that snake would dare show his face on Pride Street! Not after all he did!"

I sighed and rubbed my head as my employee threw down their rag and stomped toward the breakroom, flinging the velvet curtain aside in a huff.

Good. Maybe they'd stay back there. Dealing with Sweetheart Digs was going to be difficult enough as it was, without Yarrow throwing a fit about it.

I rubbed my temples, wishing the bottle of ibuprofen wasn't in the tiny breakroom along with Yarrow, who seemed to be slamming the cupboards back there repeatedly.

John's text had definitely come as a surprise. I'd already been gearing myself up for a night at Enrico's, but now it seemed a whole parade was heading toward my door. At least, that's what it looked like through the front windows. There were a few streaks which stood out in the sun pouring through, which made me wish I'd had Yarrow take out their frustration on the plate glass instead of that mirror.

"Hey, babe," John said, as Marsha ran ahead, yipping in excitement. Klaus looked more alert in his little cart than last time I'd seen him, so I could count that as a win, at least.

John was trailed by Tracy, Xavier, Sweetheart Digs, Ron, Fred, and Princess Sparkle Toes.

"Jacki and Bex really wanted to come but the café was slammed when we went by," John explained, as he unhooked Marsha's leash and gently lifted Klaus from the cart, settling him on a bed near one of the sofas in the Deco section before folding the cart to get it out of the way.

I sighed, gave my sweetheart a kiss, and walked over to lock the front door, flipping the sign to Closed.

Usually, I would offer guests tea or water, but I really just wanted to get whatever this was over.

Everyone was already perching on the sofa and chairs in the Deco section, even dragging a few ottomans and spare chairs over from other sections. I would have preferred we all meet further from the front windows, but it was too late now.

I stayed at the big wood sideboard we used as a front desk and cashpoint, leaning against the outside of the counter, needing some space.

"All right, Digs, spill," said Princess Sparkle Toes from her chair. Her orange lipstick was slightly smeared, which meant she was upset and distracted. I couldn't blame her.

Sweetheart Digs had lost the air of bravado he used to carry as the self-proclaimed Mayor of Pride Street. He'd dropped weight and his clothing no longer sparkled. As a matter of fact, the black chinos and white linen shirt he sported were quite subdued. Just like his energy. His dark brown hair needed a cut, and his blue eyes looked bloodshot.

I glanced at John, who was looking at Digs with a worried frown. They'd had a brief past, before my time, but Sweetheart's past behavior had put paid to any lingering affection. At least, that's what I thought. I'm far less experienced than John in matters of the heart, but my own ex, Vyviane was a case in point. Overall, I loathed her, but if she was in trouble? I'm not sure what I would do.

Sweetheart Digs cleared his throat and began.

"I was in love with Poison Penny. She stuck with me when I was in prison."

He choked up, swiped at his eyes, then cleared his throat again. "I...I was even going to propose, right before I got taken away."

"The ring!" Ron exclaimed, right as Marsha barked and Fred gave a low woof.

I swear, it was as if the animals understood.

"The ring," Sweetheart Digs agreed. "I didn't know what happened to it after I got out. I wasn't sure if anyone had found it or..."

"What about the necklaces?" Ron asked, scratching Fred absently as the black lab thumped his long, feathery tail.

"They were my memorial to Penny, after she died. I just wanted everyone in the neighborhood to remember her as she was: sparkling and beautiful. But I couldn't exactly show up at a funeral service, could I? So, I decided to mail the letter pendants to everyone."

"But then I saw you at the post office," Tracy said.

"Right," said Sweetheart Digs. "And then Xavier saw me near campus. I didn't know where you lived, but I'd heard you had the cat."

"That cat has a name," Xavier spat out. "Her name is Sapphire, and she deserves a lot better than the likes of you!"

Digs hung his head. I almost believed he was actually remorseful.

"You're right. I know I need to make amends to everyone, including Sapphire."

"I don't get it, man," Ron said. "No one even knew you and Penny were a thing, right? And you've been away for how many months? Then, right after Penny dies, and Jerome and Klaus here get poisoned, you show up? What kind of amends, exactly, do you think you'll be able to make? To anyone?"

Wow. That was quite a speech from Ron.

Sweetheart Digs sputtered a bit, then turned to me. "Can I get some water or something?"

"Later," I said. "Right now, I need to know why you're here and what you want."

Every head turned to where I leaned against the wood sideboard, shock on their faces. Yeah, like Ron, I wasn't usually the sharp-tongued one of our group, but I was tired, overwhelmed, and fed up from the heat, people dying, and everyone interrupting my workday when I had a client design I needed to finish. The corgis need their kibble, after all, and I refuse to be a kept man, no matter how well John's book sales are doing.

"We all want to know," Tracy said, sniffing as if she might burst into tears. It just goes to show that even a butch lesbian whom I always considered to be sweet but kind of badass could be overwhelmed and prone to strong emotions.

My ears buzzed with tension as we all waited for Sweetheart to explain himself.

"I'm here because Xavier caught me, frankly. But since that happened, I wanted to come clean to everyone and see if there was any way I could help."

"Help with what, exactly, you snake?" Yarrow's voice came from behind me.

"Y-yarrow!" Sweetheart Digs held his hands to his chest as if he was on the verge of a heart attack. "I didn't know you worked here."

"Come on, Sweetheart. Stop messing around." John's voice held a sharp edge now, which helped me relax a bit. My partner was taking Sweetheart Digs' transformation with a grain of salt. A large one.

Sweetheart Digs held John's steely gaze.

"I want to help find out why that jumped-up little hairdresser killed my beloved. And I want to find out why Enrico was trying to steal her away from me!"

John cut his eyes my way. They were wide with shock.

I groaned. There was no way I was getting out of going to Enrico's tonight. That much was clear.

But was Sweetheart Digs just trying to cast suspicion on Sebastian and Enrico because he was guilty himself?

And what about that suspicious hairdresser, Carla? Or one of the queens at Enrico's, like the one in the blond wig who'd almost choked me with her hairspray? And had Jerome been protecting someone, or had he just been going into kidney failure?

Whether I liked it or not, there was only one way to find out. I'd have to pull up my big boy pants, pick out a bow tie, and brace myself for Enrico's.

CHAPTER 31

Marsha

KLAUS and I were in the big bedroom at the end of the upstairs hallway. Klaus rested on our bed next to the window seat, because he was still not feeling his best. He'd been complaining about choking down the charcoal on his food, but I made sure he ate every bite because the doctor said it was important.

Now that Jerome was dead, I had to make sure Klaus didn't follow.

I trotted between the walk-in closet and the bathroom across the hall, trying to keep track of John and Garrett as they got ready to go out.

"Was Xavier able to come as backup tonight?" John was asking Garrett from the walk-in closet. "Or Princess Sparkle Toes?"

Adam sat in the window seat, one boot crossed over his knee, with the little ghost beagle curled beside him.

Garrett rummaged in the dresser, lifting a flowered bow tie out with a small grunt of satisfaction. I swear, humans are pleased by the smallest things.

"Xavier had some big event at the university tonight and Sparkle Toes said Mr. Cheeks wasn't feeling well, but really? She told me earlier she wasn't feeling too safe right now, and I bet that's what's keeping her home."

If I was Sparkle Toes, I would already be at the night-club! I hated that Garrett and John were going to Enrico's without me.

Garrett headed to the bathroom across the hall, and I turned to Klaus.

"What if they find the culprit tonight?" I whined. *"It isn't fair that we won't all be there!"*

Klaus just sighed. I growled to myself and followed Garrett, who was scowling at the bathroom mirror, putting some kind of stinky pomade on his hair and fussing with that flowered bow tie.

"Babe?" John called from the depths of the walk-in closet. "Have you seen my blue platform sandals?"

"I can't keep track of your shoes!" Garrett called back.

I knew exactly where John's shoes were. The blue sandals weren't very interesting, with not nearly enough leather to chew. Besides, I'd learned to tell the difference between super expensive shoes and ones that I'd only get into a little bit of trouble if I chewed them.

These were the expensive ones.

But I had no time for thinking about shoes right now. The humans would have to dress themselves, even if the sandals remained lost behind the laundry hamper.

I trotted back into the room, figuring if I couldn't go scare up more clues, I may as well continue my argument with Klaus.

"You know I'm right about Enrico's!" I barked. *"We're the ones who did all the work figuring this out! And has John even*

checked the poison book yet? And what about Sapphire? She could have been in danger!"

"Stop working yourself up," Klaus snapped. "You're doing my head in."

"Well, you're a…a tan potato!"

Adam lifted a hand, palm out. I knew what that meant. It meant stop arguing. But I did not want to stop! I was anxious and angry, and my friend was still sick, and another human was dead when we'd thought he was fine.

What if Klaus was not fine? What then? Was anyone thinking about that besides me?

::*Marsha. I know you want to do something, but we need Garrett and John to investigate, and you can't go to Enrico's. They probably don't even allow service animals inside.*::

"And whose rule is that? What? Disabled people can't go out to nightclubs now?" I really wanted to bite something. Maybe I'd fetch John's shoes after all…

Klaus yawned and lazily scratched an ear.

"Why don't you see if you can get John into his office, to look at that book?"

That wasn't a bad idea. But getting John into his office when he was getting dressed up was easier said than done. Maybe I could cause some sort of emergency…

But even if I could get John or Garrett to go to the office, how would I convince them to look at the book?

Garrett came back into the bedroom as I was pondering and headed for the closet.

"Did you find them?" he asked.

"No," John huffed. "I'll just have to wear something else!"

Now it was my turn to sigh. I trotted to the closet and poked my nose in.

"Marsha, not now," John said. "There isn't room for all of us in here at once."

I ignored him and headed past the shoe racks, hanging pants, and the floor-to-ceiling section filled with the bright colors of what Garrett called "John's Frocks" and began pawing at the hamper.

"Marsha, what?" Garrett came to move me, but I kept pawing and scratching.

"Oh! John! Look! Marsha found your shoes!"

"Thank you! It's nice when she's helpful for once."

"Not fair!" I barked as John reached past me for the sandals. I grabbed one in my mouth and ran.

Guess this was the emergency I was looking for.

I raced through the bedroom, sandal wedged in my jaws, with Klaus barking wildly in my wake.

"Marsha P. Johson! Get back here!" Garrett shouted. I could hear John cursing and then feet pounding down the hall.

Glancing back at Garrett, face flushed above that bow tie, glasses slipping down his nose, and John, barefoot and in a floor length emerald-green dress, I ducked into the office, parking my butt in front of the desk, right under where I remembered Adam painstakingly flipping the pages.

Garrett arrived first and crouched, motioning for the shoe.

"Drop it!" he said, trying to make his voice sound deeper.

Hah!

I growled and stood my ground.

"Marsha, if there are teeth marks on that shoe, I swear..." John said, sweeping into the room. Adam stayed in the doorway, Lucy at his feet. I could hear Klaus slowly shuffling down the long hallway.

Not so long ago, he would have bounced right after me. And that was why I had John's shoe in my mouth, wasn't it? I had to avenge my best friend, even if he is a pain in the butt.

"Come on, Marsha," Garrett said. "Drop the shoe."

Sandal still in my mouth, I stood on my back feet and pawed at the desk. My nose didn't quite clear the top, but I hoped one of them got the message.

Garret reached to grab me, and I dropped the sandal.

I saw Klaus slide to the floor in the hallway, exhausted by his short jaunt.

"Adam! Help?"

And then the ghost was at my side, doing his best to breathe across the book. I barely heard the paper rustling, but maybe it was enough.

"There's only one small tooth mark," John was saying. "I guess I can still wear this to a dark nightclub. But don't think you're off the hook, Marsha!"

John turned to sweep back out of the room.

"Adam! Talk to Garrett! Now!"

I knew communication via Adam's old ring was spotty and worked best when Garrett was making an effort to tune in, but I was getting desperate.

::Garrett. Look at the book.::

Garrett gasped, sounding startled, but finally looked down.

"John? I think you need to come back here!"

"What now? I need to finish my makeup!"

"Please?"

Something clattered on the bathroom countertop, then silence, and finally John stepped back into the office, one false eyelash on, the other eye looking practically naked next to it, despite the sparkly green eye shadow. He seemed really annoyed.

I backed up to be closer to Klaus. Adam hovered on the other side of the desk.

"Look at this," Garrett said, finger on the book.

John peered over his shoulder, then gave a low whistle.

"Damn. Formaldehyde? And what's that bookmark? I swear I didn't leave it there."

Garrett flipped back and Adam gave me a wink.

"Paraphenylenediamine?" Garrett said. "What in the world is that?"

John bent over, reading the entry. "Looks like both formaldehyde and paraphenylenediamine are chemicals used in hair salons."

Garrett's face went even paler than usual.

"The vet's office never called us about the lab results. Do you think…?"

John looked grim.

"I'd bet on it. One of those chemicals was in that conditioner bottle. It would only take a couple of teaspoons to kill someone, eventually. Thank the ancestors Klaus is okay."

"Oh!" Garrett said, rushing to gather both of us in his arms. Then he jerked as if burned.

"But John! We thought Jerome was okay, too."

"Damn. Think we should stay home?"

::*You have to go to Enrico's.*:: Adam said. ::*You have to solve this.*::

I was looking right at Adam, and Garrett followed my gaze.

"Well then, Adam, you and Marsha have to make sure

Klaus is okay while we're gone. At the first sign anything is wrong, you set this ring on fire!"

Garrett held up the hand with Adam's ring on it, looking as fierce as I'd ever seen him.

"We'll keep Klaus safe!" I barked. *"Promise!"*

"Guess we'd better get to the club," Garrett said. "And put a stop to this, once and for all."

CHAPTER 32

Garrett

AH, Enrico's. At least I was dressed more like myself, which was hard to do when one is a dandy battling summer heat. Dressing for summer always makes me feel uneasy.

Tonight's only problem—besides heading to a crowded club to investigate two murders—was that John towered over me in those blue strappy heels. It's funny, I didn't mind our height difference when John was in butch mode, but I guess I have enough internalized gender normativity to feel slightly strange when a femme presenting person is so much taller than I am.

Despite decades of work on gender equality and liberation, men are still culturally expected to be taller than women, which is a ridiculous expectation for a queer trans man to have, but here we are.

I ignored my discomfort and held John's hand in mine, grateful for the earplugs with their festive rose-gold tinted ring that winked from inside my ear. They picked up some of the flowers in my tie.

Once I'd figured out that cutting certain decibels of

noise helped my brain, navigating social situations had become much easier. It still wasn't pleasant but made it possible for me to enjoy a night out with my partner.

Not that either of us were looking forward to being out tonight. As a matter of fact, I was kind of surprised John had wanted to go in drag. That seemed like a lot of effort for a murder investigation. On the other hand, if we had to talk to any of the performers, it might set them at ease.

But first, the bar. Then to find Enrico.

Ace was not her usual swaggering, smirky self. Her head, which had been gleamingly smooth last time I saw her, now had the shadow of hair growth. Her posture was more slumped, and she was serving drinks like an automaton, not a person who loved a crowd.

"Let's wait on those drinks," John murmured in my ear. "Ace doesn't look ready to talk about anything."

I looked up at my gorgeous sweetheart, who had decided against a wig tonight, styling the longer hair on top of his head into gentle waves, kind of 1930s style.

Nodding in response, I scanned the crowded club. The current performer on stage was dressed as a cowgirl, if that cowgirl was Beyoncé on a budget, lip synching to what I thought was Shania Twain.

"Enrico!" John said, flipping a hand toward the right of the stage, near the hallway that led to the green room.

I tugged his hand, leading him between the people standing and watching the performer, and the tables and booths on their risers further back. But before we got to Enrico, the performer finished her act, and the DJ started up again. This meant a large percentage of the people who'd been standing around surged toward the dance floor in front of the stage, crossing my path. Some people began dancing in place, waving their arms around.

John jerked me back from one flailing hand right before it clocked me in the glasses.

"Let me," John said, taking the lead. I followed along like an imprinted baby duck, all of a sudden grateful for John's taller frame and heels. The extra height helped him keep track of Enrico and to cut a swathe through the dancing, laughing crowd.

It was nice feeling slightly protected. Even though I was still getting bumped, I wasn't in danger of losing my glasses anymore.

It seemed to take forever, even though the DJ was still on the same thumping song by the time we reached Enrico.

The nightclub owner looked as terrible as Ace. All of this must be taking a toll on him. He also seemed tipsy, the golden skin of his handsome face flushed with drink, dark eyes bloodshot. That was really disturbing. I'd never known him to be a big drinker. The most he ever had was a couple of fingers of good whiskey and that was it for the night.

"Can we talk to you?" John said over the music and the crowd.

Enrico gave a sharp nod, and led us toward the back wall, gesturing to a few regulars to clear the booth they were in.

A booth on the far edge of the dance floor isn't private in a visual sense, but for conversation? It would be as good as Enrico's office. Better, in fact, because us disappearing upstairs right now might raise suspicion.

Not that I thought the killer was in the nightclub, but frankly? I couldn't be sure.

John and I slid across the red Naugahyde, across the bend of the curved bench from the club owner. I fingered

Adam's ring, trying to soothe myself, and also ready for any communication the ghost might need.

"How are you holding up?" John asked.

Enrico pursed his lips and shook his head. Holding back tears.

Dang. What was that about?

"Should we go to your office?" I asked. If Enrico was going to sit here and cry, maybe having this conversation where people could see us wasn't the best idea after all.

"No. This is fine. I'll be fine."

"Enrico," I said, leaning across the table. "What's wrong? Is it Jerome?"

For all I knew he and Jerome had a relationship beyond employer and bartender.

He shook his head again, sniffing loudly. I reached into my back pocket and pulled out a clean handkerchief, which I handed over.

"Thanks." He blew his nose. "I may as well tell you, because all of this is going to come out eventually and if… if it helps you solve the case, well…"

But he didn't say anything more, just stared out over the crowd with a lost look on his face.

"Enrico?" John prodded gently. "What's going on?"

"I was in love with Henry."

His voice was so soft, it barely carried across the table. John and I scooted closer, leaning as far across the table as we could without crawling on top of it.

"Henry?" I asked. "You mean Poison Penny?"

Enrico waved a hand as if swiping away a fly.

"Yeah. Sure. Penny. Penny was a terrific performer. One of my best. But it wasn't really her that I fell for. It who she was offstage. Who he was. Henry. I'd given him a ring and everything."

John and I shared a look. The ring.

"What happened?" John asked.

"I… I'm not sure. I thought we were happy. But then Henry said he lost the ring. A diamond. Not cheap. I thought maybe he was getting cold feet, but he insisted that wasn't it at all. So, we carried on. Long engagement and all that."

"And then?" I asked.

Enrico shuddered and held the handkerchief over his eyes. His shoulders were shaking as the tears came in earnest.

"And then she died," he said. "And now Jerome is gone, too. And I don't know what to do."

I exhaled a breath I hadn't even realized I was holding. My brain tried to slot this new information in along with the clues and facts and suspicions swirling there.

As John patted Enrico's hand, I noticed the music had stopped. The DJ was announcing the next performer.

Edie. The 1960s style drag queen who'd almost choked and blinded me with her hairspray.

She stepped onto the stage to the beat of an old Deee-Lite song from the early 1990s, her thin body encased in an op-art wild patterned jumpsuit. A single spotlight lit up her blond wig like the sun.

And then she turned our way, and I got a good look at her face. I gasped, a hand flying to my mouth. Her eyes widened in surprise.

Edie was Rex, the assistant at Sebastian's salon. I bolted out of the booth, barely hearing John and Enrico calling after me in confusion. I had to get to her.

But it was already too late. Edie threw down her microphone and fled the stage. But she wasn't racing toward the green room, no.

She ran pell-mell, arms pumping, through the confused crowd.

Edie was aiming for the front door, and there was no way my short legs were going to catch her before she disappeared.

CHAPTER 33

Marsha

JOHN AND GARRETT had left Klaus and I curled in a big floor bed near the fireplace in case Klaus needed food or water while they were gone.

I was in a light doze when Klaus nudged me.

"Someone is on the porch," he woofed softly.

I woke from my doze in a rush and bounded toward the window, shoving the curtains aside with my nose.

A friendly face stared back at me and tapped the glass. Oh, good. It was just Xavier! Maybe he'd come with news. I just hoped John and Garrett were okay.

::*Who is it?*:: Adam asked, rising from the couch.

"It's Xavier! But…" My brain scrambled itself for a second. *"But there's no way to let him inside!"*

Dang.

"Didn't he help us once when John was out of town and Garrett was sick? Maybe he still has a key," Klaus reminded us just as a knock came at the door, followed by the turning of said key.

I was at the door in a flash, but Xavier was already inside and toeing off his shoes.

"Hey there, Marsha!"

"What are you doing here?" I barked.

He bent to pat my head, but I shied away. If he had bad news about John and Garrett, I wanted to get it over with.

"It's okay, girl. Don't be worried. Garrett sent me here."

"What? Why?"

He was already gathering up my leash, then poked his head in to check on Klaus.

Adam blocked his way, arms crossed over his chest, boots spread.

"Why is it so cold in here?" Xavier asked, shoving through the ghost.

Adam stomped silently after him, looking concerned, then paused, head tilted like Klaus and I do when we're listening really hard.

Oh! Garrett must be talking to him! My tail wagged in excitement.

::It's okay, Marsha. Garrett just needs your help.::

"What?" I yelped, heart pounding. *"What happened?"*

"Sorry you can't come with us buddy," Xavier was saying to Klaus. "It isn't safe for you. But Garrett needs our help to track down someone on the streets."

"What?" Klaus woofed in alarm. *"Who?"*

Xavier looked from Klaus to me and shook his head.

"I swear, sometimes I think you two speak more English than you ought to be able to. There's a performer on the loose, and Garrett is convinced she's the killer."

"Then what are we waiting for?" I barked, jumping up and down on my front paws. *"Harness me up and let's go!"*

Leaving Klaus behind was hard, but a corgi's gotta do what a corgi's gotta do. What kind of a detective would I be if I passed up this chance? Besides, Garrett said he needed me.

Me.

"Do you know what we're looking for?" Xavier asked, as I tugged on my leash, eagerly sniffing my way through the dark residential area, heading for the lights of Pride Street. "Garrett said Edie was wearing a bright jumpsuit, but he also said Edie is a man called Rex who works at the salon. So, maybe you've smelled this person before?"

"That's easy!" I barked, not breaking my stride. It didn't matter if Sebastian was fresh from a shower, he still carried a lingering scent from the salon. I bet this Edie/Rex person was the same.

At least, I hoped so.

We moved swiftly through the dark streets, but so far, nothing out of the ordinary. Just some cats and opossum scents, mingled with the occasional raccoon and the smell of dog pee from everyone's walks earlier in the evening. The streets here were pretty empty, with barely even any cars driving by. Not as deserted as winter, but empty enough.

I wondered how exactly Garrett expected us to find this person. I mean, what if Edie/Rex had gotten into a car? They would be long gone by now.

"Garrett just texted again," Xavier said. "He and John are halfway up Pride Street now and Garrett thinks we should wind our way there. Maybe you can sniff some of the side streets? But I also wonder if Edie didn't duck into a different business. All the restaurants should be closing soon, but maybe Axle's Bar? They'll be open!"

"Good idea! Let's go there!"

I tugged my leash, heading off the side streets. If this person had gone down one, there was no telling which one. That route could take us forever. Besides, humans like this Edie probably liked the cover of other humans, so a bar was more likely than wandering the dark streets alone.

"Okay! I guess you like the idea of Axle's better than combing the side streets like Garrett said. And I'm clearly just along for a ride on the Marsha train."

He muttered that last sentence, but my superior canine hearing picked it up.

Swinging onto Pride Street, we were soon in the thick of things. Even though Xavier was right and most businesses were closed this late at night, plenty of people were still around. Bruiser's was locked up tight, but further down across the street, I saw the lights on at Bones, Dogs, and Harmony.

I tugged at Xavier to cross.

"Marsha! Don't yank! There's a car coming!"

Fine. We waited until the coast was clear and were at Ron and Fred's shop soon enough.

I could see Ron inside, closing up. He'd just clipped a leash on Fred and held out his arm for Josephine Baker to climb aboard.

Barking and pawing at the heavy glass door, I waited for Ron to notice us.

The locks chunked and Ron yanked the door open.

"Bad dog!" Josephine Baker squawked.

"Xavier? Marsha? What are you doing here?"

"*Do you need help?*" Fred asked, his soft ears in their alert mode, tail waiting to decide whether it should wag or not.

"*Yes!*" I barked. "*We're on the hunt for a possible killer!*"

"Garrett and John are chasing one of Enrico's performers. Might be the killer," Xavier was saying. "We were headed to Axle's to see if they ducked in there."

"Let's go, then," Ron replied as Fred surged onto the

sidewalk. "Though I don't know if they'll let the animals inside. And Josephine here might cause a ruckus."

He locked the door. Why did he have so many locks? *Ka-chunk! Ka-chunk! Ka-chunk!*

Finally, we were on our way, racing down the sidewalk as quickly as old Fred's legs could go. The lab was slower than I was, but his legs were longer, so that helped, at least.

We got to How We Roll, where they were cleaning up the outside patio. Axle's was right across the street, but Ron and Xavier made us stop to make sure there wasn't traffic.

Music and people poured out onto Axle's patio from the big open doors leading inside. It stank like weird vape juice, spilled alcohol, and a bewildering array of human body odor and cologne.

How in the world was a dog supposed to sniff out hair salon chemicals in this olfactory mess?

CHAPTER 34

Garrett

JOHN WAS CURSING at his heels, and I was never more glad to be a dandy instead of going high femme.

The bouncer outside Enrico's had been quite distressed when she'd realized a possible killer had gotten away. But when she pointed us in the general direction of our house, I knew just what needed to happen.

Luckily, Xavier should be en-route home from his event at the college. When I texted him, he said he was right near our house!

There was no telling whether he and Marsha could catch Edie, but the chance of trapping her between two parties was better than John and I going it alone.

"Should we stop along the way?" John asked. "I mean, Edie could have jumped into a ride share, or she ducked down a side street, but…"

"Xavier and Marsha are scoping out the side streets."

I looked around Pride Street. What was even open? Then I remembered the match book I'd picked up in Enrico's dressing room what felt like a month ago even though it had only been a few days.

"Axle's. We should check there. It's on our way home, anyway."

Better yet, it was only half a block away.

"Ron?" John said, when we got to the patio. "What are you doing here?"

"Xavier and Marsha came to get us. They're inside." He jerked his head to the LED-lit interior filled with dancing, drinking people. I could see why Fred and Josephine wouldn't want to go inside.

As it was, Josephine Baker was singing half the parts to what sounded like a Lil Nas X song, much to the amusement of some of the patio patrons, who egged her on.

"What a zoo," John muttered. Somehow, I knew he wasn't talking about the actual animals.

I re-set my fancy earplugs and braced myself for the onslaught of a nightclub that was exponentially worse than Enrico's as far as sensory overload.

The things I do to help our community, I swear.

I let my tall partner take the lead again, cutting a swathe through the crowd. This had its drawbacks, of course, because John is gorgeous whether he's going butch or femme, and several people wanted to "talk" to him en-route.

He smiled politely and forged ahead.

Tugging on his hand to slow him down, I went up on my toes and shouted near his ear.

"Do you see Xavier? Or, you know?"

I didn't want to say Edie's voice out loud, just in case she was within hearing distance. Unlikely in all the brouhaha, but better safe than sorry.

John shook his head and kept going.

"Wait!" I tugged again. "Is that barking?"

His head snapped to the right and sure enough, there was Marsha's distinctive bark, followed by a sharp yip.

Blood rushed to my face, and I shoved through the crowd, taking the lead. Someone better not be hurting Marsha!

"Excuse me!" I called out periodically, just to be polite, following Marsha's voice.

And then I saw Xavier and Edie, shoved into a corner near a high standing table with a glossy white top that I just knew was sticky with a night's worth of booze.

Marsha was growling at Edie, shoulders poised as if she was about to bite.

Then the crowd in front of me parted suddenly, and I stumbled, with John catching my shoulder before I barreled into Xavier's back.

Edie's dark rimmed eyes grew wide as she saw me over Xavier's shoulder. She shoved him out of the way, but Marsha pivoted, tripping Edie who, arms pinwheeling, began to fall.

Right onto me.

I ducked, bracing my shoulders which hit her chest. With a sharp "oof!" she was draped across my back, her velocity sending us both into a sprawl onto the filthy, sticky floor, Marsha barking and growling wildly, Xavier and John shouting in alarm.

My cheek felt like it was stuck to the floor and my nice trousers would need the dry cleaner. Yuck.

"Some help please?" I muttered. I don't think John or Xavier heard me, but Edie did.

"I would have gotten away with it if it weren't for you and your meddling dogs! Enrico would have been mine!"

"What?" I jerked, pushing myself off the disgusting floor as John and Xavier hoisted Edie off my back.

"That bitch Poison Penny already had Sweetheart Digs! Why did she need Enrico, too? Greedy guts! Stringing them both along for the past two years!"

A small crowd around us finally seemed to figure out something was going on.

"Did she just say she killed Poison Penny?" a voice asked over the pulsing music.

"Sweetheart Digs?" said another voice. "I thought he was in prison…"

I barely heard the comments, my eyes focused on Edie. Half her makeup had smeared off, revealing angry blotches across her face and neck.

"You're confessing to killing Penny?" I asked.

Edie's teeth snapped shut, her mouth set in a mulish line.

"Let's get her out of here," John said over my head. "Xavier?"

Xavier handed me Marsha's leash and grabbed one of Edie's arms. She tried to yank free, but John grabbed the other.

"I'm being kidnapped!" she bellowed. "Someone help me!"

The small crew around us laughed.

"Sounds like you're about to get your comeuppance, queen!" called another drag queen.

"You two need help?" A Latine man in a tight white singlet and even tighter jeans asked. He had muscles for days.

"That'd be great," I replied, figuring John and Xavier could use all the help they could get.

"Where are we going?" the man asked, taking Edie's arm from John and motioning my sweetheart to lead the way.

John looked at me.

"Enrico's," I said.

I needed the full story before we decided what to do, and since Edie had just professed her twisted love for the club owner, it seemed like just the place to get to the bottom of it all.

CHAPTER 35

Marsha

I WAS EXHAUSTED. Sitting next to two pushed-together four-top picnic tables outside Bruiser's Best Beans, it was all I could do to keep up with the conversation between the humans, plus fill the animals in on what had gone on.

"So, we cornered Edie in the bar!" I barked. *"And when she tried to escape, I tripped her!"*

"You are a brave dog," Fred woofed. *"I would have helped you if Ron had let us go inside."*

"I know, Fred. I know."

Much as I enjoyed being the hero of the hour, I really wanted a nap, like Mr. Cheeks.

Huddled over the tabletop, clutching a coffee cup, Garrett looked about how I felt. Neither of us were used to late nights. But at least it wasn't blazing hot!

Everyone was out, enjoying the weather as if two people hadn't died. But that's the way life is, isn't it? The rest of us go on. At least Klaus looked more perky today. Even though he needed another check up from the vet, the doctor thought he was in the clear.

Speaking of everyone, gathered around the tables were Sebastian, who looked troubled, Princess Sparkle Toes sitting next to him, looking relieved, with Mr. Cheeks napping quietly in his pink ventilated hamster purse, Ron, Xavier, Charles, and John and Garrett, of course. Both Bex and Jackie took turns between customers to come outside for news.

Fred, Bruiser, Klaus and me were arrayed around the humans, on the sidewalk around the tables. Even Sapphire was here, up on a bench near us, in a spot between Xavier and Charles. She was tethered inside her soft carrier with the side and top open so she could talk while still ensconced on her cushion.

It felt good to be surrounded by friends.

"So, let me get this straight," Charles was saying.

"You're not going to get a *straight* answer from anyone at this table," Sparkle Toes said. Everyone laughed, including Charles.

"Point taken," the older man said with a smile. "But this Edie or Rex person was in love with Enrico? And Enrico was engaged to Poison Penny who was also dating Sweetheart Digs?"

The whole thing made my head swim.

"Human relationships are so complicated," Klaus yipped.

Wasn't that the truth? I especially didn't understand why humans spent so much time with people they said they didn't like. Or seemed to love and hate each other at the same time.

I either like a dog or don't like a dog. Simple. But maybe that's just me.

"Enrico proposed to Henry Templeton," Xavier replied. "And Sweetheart was in love with his Poison Penny persona. They dated a bit before he went to jail, and I guess the two of them corresponded while Sweetheart Digs was inside, but that supposedly stopped after Henry and Enrico got engaged... At least, that's what Enrico said."

"But how did Sapphire get the ring then?" Ron asked, then took a sip of coffee while he waited. Drinking. Good idea.

I lapped some water from one of the sidewalk bowls Bex had just refilled, then lay back down with a sigh.

"Enrico thinks Edie stole it from Penny at the club," Xavier continued. "Rex had two part-time jobs besides performing as Edie at Enrico's, one at Sebastian's and the other at the grooming parlor. He must have hidden it in Sapphire's collar, planning to retrieve it next time we took her in."

"He did!" Sapphire meowed. *"But no one would listen to me when I complained about it bothering me!"*

The fluffy gray cat cut her eyes up at Xavier and Charles. Xavier reached down to scratch her head and she settled back down.

I hadn't realized Rex worked at the grooming parlor, too, because Klaus and I rarely need it. If only I'd known, this case could have been solved much more quickly!

"I bet he thought he could sell the ring or something," Sebastian said around a mouthful of coffee cake. "He was always hard up for money, and always talking about having big plans... but he never actually said what they were."

"Enrico said Rex/Edie had been making noise about wanting a partnership, but Enrico didn't take her seriously."

"Just like he didn't take her seriously when she

professed her love, either," John said. "I bet people get crushes on Enrico all the time."

"Do you understand any of this?" Bruiser asked.

"I sure don't," Klaus yipped. *"I've spent most of the past few days sleeping and am really confused now!"*

Because my friend was still recovering, I was polite and didn't comment that Klaus was often confused.

"It's a love thing," Fred woofed. *"Ron says it makes a lot of humans do things they shouldn't."*

That was the truth!

Jacki came out and hovered, clearing some coffee cups and plates, but I could tell she was really there to listen.

"The upshot is," Garrett interjected, "That Rex/Edie decided Poison Penny had to go. And Jerome grew suspicious, so he had to go, too. Edie claims she didn't mean to kill anyone, she just thought Penny would get sick and quit the club."

"But Penny died!" Sebastian's voice was ragged. "How could Rex poison Jerome after that?"

"He thought the second dose was small enough. It's why Jerome lingered, I guess," John said, keeping his voice gentle as if he was soothing an upset animal.

Garrett handed Sebastian a handkerchief and the salon owner mopped at his face and blew his nose.

"Has anyone talked to Ace?" Jacki asked, pausing with her tray of dirty cups.

"We saw her last night," Garrett said. "She wasn't looking so good, and said she'd be taking time off. Enrico might even close temporarily. It's all a bit up in the air."

"But she could probably use a friend," said Xavier.

Jacki nodded, then headed back into the café.

We could all use friends. I gave Klaus's nose a lick. He looked surprised and pleased.

Then he licked me back.

CHAPTER 36

Garrett

JOHN and I walked home from the café, the dogs walking sedately ahead of us. Well, Klaus walked sedately. Marsha bounced from front stoop to bushes and back to Klaus, tail wagging, nose sniffing everything.

But I noticed she didn't tug on the leash or run faster than Klaus was walking. That made me smile. Marsha P. Johnson might be a brash girl and a bit gruff at times, but she cared about Klaus Nomi.

Sometimes I wondered if the ghosts of the two gay icons thought it was weird that decades after their passing, two queer men had named dogs in their honor. I hoped they would like it.

Speaking of ghosts…

"Adam really helped out again," I said. "Calling the labs with the information about the poisons this morning helped speed up the process. Too bad it's too late to help Penny or Jerome. But at least now we know…"

John nodded, then reached out and grabbed my hand.

"The thing we still don't know is who left the note on our front porch? About Xavier? They helped, too."

He was right, and I'd completely forgotten about the note after Klaus was poisoned.

"I bet it was a stylist in Sebastian's salon. Carla. There was someone I thought was a suspect for a while, because she was always glaring at me, but I think she goes part time to Portland State. She must have suspected something too and been trying to help."

Marsha gamboled toward some flowering bushes, snapping at the bees buzzing around.

"Marsha!" John's voice cracked a warning. "That's a good way to get your snoot stung!"

But the black tri-colored corgi had already moved on to an old French fry wrapper on the sidewalk.

"It would have been nice if she'd said something, instead of dropping that note."

I felt John shrug. "Some people are too afraid to get closely involved."

"And that's the cause of so many problems in the world, isn't it?"

We walked a bit in silence before turning the corner. Almost home.

As we approached the clean, sturdy lines of our gorgeous Craftsman style home, I thought back to Adam.

"Should we make some extra offerings at Adam's altar?" I asked. "To thank him for his help?"

I deferred to John in such matters. He was the one who'd grown up tending an ancestor shrine, and it had been one of the first things he set up when we got our house.

"That would be a good thing. I bet he'd like a beer."

The dogs bounced up the front steps to the broad wood porch.

John stopped me before he unlocked the front door, gently cupping my jaw with one hand.

"But you know what I bet he'd like even more?"

His eyebrows raised in question, lips smirking down at me.

I smacked his shoulder. "Great! Just what I needed! The thought of a ghost watching when…"

John just laughed and opened the door.

There was no better sound in the world.

CHAPTER 37
Adam

GARRETT AND JOHN had poured a glass of beer and
set it on the narrow table near the entryway that held my
leather hat and some framed photos and newspaper clip-
pings, along with Lucy's collar. Those photos used to be
upstairs in the bedroom, until John had declared I needed
my own shrine, not just a dresser top next to all their stuff.

I didn't mind either way. I liked being amongst the
jumble of their lives, but having my own space? That
showed how much they cared, which was nice.

Then the two men disappeared upstairs, the dogs left
sleeping in the living room because Klaus still felt too
weak to climb up and down the stairs on his own steam.

It had been decades since I'd felt the tart, slightly effer-
vescence of a beer cross my lips and tongue. Even longer
since a man's lips had touched mine. The memory of both
had not faded.

I tried the beer. I couldn't pick up the full glass, of
course. It was too heavy. But leaning forward, I could
almost smell and taste the essence of the pale amber liquid
as it wafted up toward my face.

::*It's nice*,:: I said to Lucy, who panted happily near my boots. ::*But it isn't the same.*::

Nothing was the same for me, but… I felt happiness upstairs. Garrett kissing John. Then, the smaller man must have taken off my ring. I felt the clink inside me as it dropped into the dish where he kept treasured things.

I smiled. Garrett liked his privacy, and I didn't blame him.

Much as I missed life, I felt grateful that the two men and their little dogs had accepted me as part of the family. I'd been lonely all those years, drifting in and out of consciousness, barely tethered to this realm, but not able to move anywhere else.

The walls of this house still chafed a bit sometimes, but it no longer felt like such a trap, being here. Besides, the sharp pang of emotion that used to stab at me all the time was blunted now, and that was okay by me.

I had something that many humans never did, especially humans like that Edie.

For now, at least, I was content.

———

Garrett's old nemesis shows up with a request that sends our intrepid crew on a wild chase through the world of opera, theater, intrigue and crime... Find out what happens next in Dandy Distress!

Acknowledgments

Big Thanks to my Kickstarter backers!

Thank you to Bonnie for reading, Annie for editing, and to my chosen family for years of support.

Most of all, thank you to everyone who fell in love with a couple of corgis and their friends!

By Wind

By Sea

By Moon

By Sun

By Dusk

By Dark

By Witch's Mark

The Panther Chronicles (Complete)

To Raise a Clenched Fist to the Sky

To Wrest Our Bodies From the Fire

To Drown This Fury in the Sea

To Stand With Power on This Ground

The Steel Clan Saga

We Seek No Kings

We Heed No Laws

We Ride at Night

Short Story Collections

A Hint of Faery

A Touch of Faery

A Spark of Magic

A Flame for Yuletide

A Hope for Winter

A Time for Magic

A Speculation of Stars

A Speculation of Hope

A Speculation of Time

Risk It All: Queer Stories of Love, Suspense, And Daring

Thresholds: Queer Stories of Love, Suspense, And Daring

Ghost Talker

Cats and Other Creatures

NON-FICTION

You are the Spell

Sigil Magic for Writers, Artists, & Other Creatives

Crafting a Daily Practice

Resistance Matters

Evolutionary Witchcraft

Kissing the Limitless

Make Magic of Your Life

About the Author

T. Thorn Coyle worked in many strange and diverse occupations before settling in to write books full time.

Author of the *Seashell Cove Paranormal Mystery* series, the *Pride Street Paranormal Cozy Mysteries*, *The Mouse Thief Fantasy Capers*, *The Steel Clan Saga*, *The Witches of Portland*, and *The Panther Chronicles*, Thorn's multiple non-fiction books include *Sigil Magic for Writers, Artists & Other Creatives*, *Kissing the Limitless*, *Make Magic of Your Life*, and *Evolutionary Witchcraft*. Thorn's work also appears in many anthologies, magazines, and collections.

An interloper to the Pacific Northwest U.S., Thorn drinks a lot of tea, pays proper tribute to the neighborhood cats, and talks to crows, squirrels, and trees.

Connect with Thorn:
www.thorncoyle.com

www.ingramcontent.com/pod-product-compliance
Lightning Source LLC
Chambersburg PA
CBHW070503200726
48293CB00007B/2360